Precepts in Pr

or, Stories Illustrating th

A. L. O. E.

Alpha Editions

This edition published in 2024

ISBN 9789361479045

Design and Setting By

Alpha Editions
www.alphaedis.com

Email - info@alphaedis.com

Contents

Preface.

Dear young friends (perhaps I may rather welcome some amongst you as *old* friends), I would once more gather you around me to listen to my simple stories. I have in each one endeavoured to exemplify some truth taught by the wise King Solomon, in the Book of Proverbs. Perhaps the holy words, which I trust that many of you have already learned to love, may be more forcibly imprinted on your minds, and you may apply them more to your own conduct, when you see them illustrated by tales describing such events as may happen to yourselves.

May the Giver of all good gifts make the choice of Solomon also yours; may you, each and all, be endowed with that wisdom from on high which is *more precious than rubies*; and may you find, as you proceed onward to that better home to which Heavenly Wisdom would guide you, that *her ways are ways of pleasantness, and all her paths are peace.*

A. L. O. E.

CHAPTER I.
THE TWO SONS.

"A wise son maketh a glad father: but a foolish man despiseth his mother."—PROV. xv. 20.

It was a clear, cold morning in December. Not a cloud was in the sky, and the sun shone brightly, gilding the long icicles that hung from the eaves, and gleaming on the frozen surface of the lake, as though he would have melted them by his kindly smile. But the cold was too intense for that; there was no softening of the ice; no drop hung like a tear from the glittering icicles. Alas! that we should ever find in life hearts colder and harder still, that even kindness fails to melt!

Many persons were skating over the lake—sometimes darting forward with the swiftness of the wind, then making graceful curves to the right or the left, and forming strange figures on the ice. And there were many boys also enjoying themselves as much, although in a different way—sliding along the slippery surface, and making the air ring with their merry laughter.

THE FROZEN LAKE.

One of the gayest of these last was a rosy-cheeked boy, who looked as though care or sorrow had never traced a line on his face. He had just made a very long slide, and stood flushed with the exercise to watch his companions follow him on the glistening line, when Dr. Merton, a medical man, who was taking his morning walk, and had come to the lake to see the skating, lightly touched the boy on the shoulder.

"Paul Fane, is your mother better to-day?"

"Oh, she's well enough—that's to say, she's always ailing," replied the boy carelessly, still keeping his eye upon the sliders.

"Did she sleep better last night?"

"Oh, really, why I don't exactly know. I've not seen her yet this morning."

"Not seen her!" repeated Dr. Merton in surprise.

"Oh, sir, I knew that she'd be worrying me about my coming here upon the ice. She's so fidgety and frightened—she treats one like a child, and is always fancying that there is danger when there is none;" and the boy turned down his lip with a contemptuous expression.

"I should say that you are in danger now," said Dr. Merton, very gravely.

"How so? the ice is thick enough to roast an ox upon," replied Paul, striking it with his heel.

"In danger of the anger of that great Being who hath said, *Honour thy father and thy mother*—in danger of much future pain and regret, when the time for obeying that command shall be lost to you for ever."

Paul's cheek grew redder at these words. He felt half inclined to make an insolent reply; but there was something in the doctor's manner which awed even his proud and unruly spirit.

"Where is your brother Harry?" inquired Dr. Merton.

"Oh, I suppose at home," replied Paul bluffly, glad of any change in the conversation; and still more glad was he when the gentleman turned away, and left him to pursue his amusement.

And where was Harry on that bright, cheerful morning, while his brother was enjoying himself upon the ice? In a little, dull, close room, with a peevish invalid, the sunshine mostly shut out by the dark blinds, while the sound of merry voices from without contrasted with the gloomy stillness within. Harry glided about with a quiet step, trimmed the fire, set on the kettle, prepared the gruel for his mother, and carried it gently to the side of her bed. He arranged the pillows comfortably for the sufferer, and tended her even as she had tended him in the days of his helpless infancy. The fretfulness of the sick woman never moved his patience. He remembered how often, when he was a babe, his cry had broken her rest and disturbed her comfort. How could he do enough for her who had given him life, and watched over him and loved him long, long before he had been able even to make the small return of a grateful look? Oh! what a holy thing is filial obedience! God commands it, God has blessed it, and He will bless it for ever. He that disobeys or neglects a parent is planting thorns for his own pillow, and they are thorns that shall one day pierce him even to the soul.

HARRY TENDING HIS MOTHER.

"Where is Paul?" said Mrs. Fane with uneasiness. "I am always anxious about that dear boy. I do trust that he has not ventured upon the ice."

"I believe, mother, that the ice has been considered safe, quite safe, for the last three days."

"You know nothing about the matter," cried the fretful invalid. "I had a cousin drowned once in that lake when every one said that there was no danger. I have forbidden you both a thousand times to go near the ice;" and she gave her son a look of displeasure, as though he had been the one to break her command.

"Will you not take your gruel now?" said Harry, again drawing her attention to it, and placing yet closer to her that which he had so carefully made.

"I do not like it—it's cold—it's full of lumps; you never do anything well!"

"I must try and improve," said her son, struggling to look cheerful, but feeling the task rather hard. "If you will not take this, shall I get you a little tea?"

Mrs. Fane assented with a discontented air, and Harry instantly proceeded to make some; while all the time that he was thus engaged his poor mother continued in a tone of anxiety and sorrow to express her fears for her elder son.

"Are you more comfortable now, dear mother?" said Harry, after she had partaken of her nice cup of tea. Her only reply was a moan. "Can I do anything else for you?—yes, I see; the top of that blind hangs loose, and the light comes in on your eyes; I will set it right in a minute!" and he jumped lightly on a chair to reach it.

His mother followed him with her eyes—her deep, sunken eyes. Gradually the moisture gathered in them, as she looked at her dutiful son; for, fretful and unreasonable towards him as illness might sometimes make her, she yet dearly loved him, and felt his value. When he returned to her side, these eyes were still fixed upon him; she feebly pressed his hand, and murmured, "You are my comfort, Harry!"

And there was another Eye beholding with love that obedient and dutiful child! He who was once subject to an earthly parent, who cared for her even amid the agonies of the Cross—He looked approvingly down upon the true-hearted boy, who was filling the post assigned him by his Lord—who was letting his light shine in his home!

The red sun was setting before Paul returned; for, heedless of the fears to which his absence might give rise, he had taken his noonday meal with a neighbour. It was not that he did not really love his fond mother, but he loved himself a great deal more. He had never chosen to consider obedience as a sacred duty, and irreverence towards a parent as a sin. He never dreamed of sacrificing his will to hers; and a smile or a kiss to his mother, when he had been more than usually selfish or rude, had hitherto been sufficient to quiet the boy's conscience, and, as he said, "make all right between them." But wounds are not so easily healed, a parent's claims are not so easily set aside, and the hour had now come when Paul was to feel the thorns which he had planted for himself.

DR. MERTON AND PAUL.

"I shall have a precious scold from mother," muttered the boy half aloud, as he approached the door, "for going on the ice, and staying out all day. I should like to know what is the use of a holiday, if I am not to spend it as I like? I would rather be in school than moping away my time at home like Harry! I wish that I were old enough to go and enlist, and be out of hearing of mother's endless chiding!"

"You will never hear it again," said the solemn voice of one just quitting the door as Paul came up to it. He started to see Dr. Merton.

"What is the matter?" cried Paul, a strange feeling of fear and awe coming over his heart.

"Your poor mother, about two hours ago, was taken with an alarming fit—I dare hardly give hopes that she will see the morning!"

Paul stayed to hear no more, but rushed into the house. One of the neighbours was there, who had kindly offered to stay that night to help Harry to nurse his dying parent. The young boy was now praying beside her bed—praying for his mother on earth to his Father in heaven!

Paul went up to the bed, cold, trembling with his emotions. He gazed in anguish on the altered features of one whose love he had so ill repaid. Mrs. Fane lay unconscious of all that passed—unconscious of the bitter tears shed by her sons. She no longer could rejoice in the affection of the one, or be stung by the neglect of the other. Oh! what would not Paul have given, as he hung over her now, for one forgiving look from those closed eyes! What would he not have given to have heard those pale lips speak, even though it had been but to chide! But his grief and his fears now came too late—his mother never spoke again!

In a few days both the boys stood by the open grave, and no one who had seen the sorrow of both, without being aware of the former circumstances of their lives, would have known what different recollections filled their hearts—like poison in the bleeding wound of one, soothing balm in that of his brother! "My last act towards my mother was that of disobedience—her last feeling towards me was of displeasure and pain! I clouded, perhaps I shortened her life; and the anger of my God is upon me!" Such were the thoughts of Paul—his agonizing thoughts—as he heard the earth fall on the coffin of her who had loved him best upon earth. But not for untold wealth would Harry have exchanged the remembrance of his parent's last fond look, her last sweet words to him. "Harry, you are my comfort!" sounded in his ears as though an angel had repeated it to the mourner.

THE FUNERAL.

And not then alone, but when time had softened his sorrow—yes, even through the long course of his honoured, useful life, if care weighed on his heart, he thought of those words, and they lightened his burden of care; when joy elated his spirit, they yet brightened that joy—his mother's blessing seemed for ever resting upon him! *Honour thy father and mother: that thy days may be long upon the land which the Lord thy God giveth thee. A wise son maketh a glad father: but a foolish man despiseth his mother.*

He makes his mother sad,

The proud, unruly child,

Who will not brook

Her warning look,

Nor hear her counsels mild.

He makes his mother sad,
Who, in his thoughtless mirth,
Can e'er forget
His mighty debt
To her who gave him birth.

He makes his mother sad,
Who turns from Wisdom's way;
Whose stubborn will,
Rebelling still,
Refuses to obey.

He makes his mother sad—
And sad his lot must prove:
A mother's fears,
A mother's tears,
Are marked by God above!

Oh! who so sad as he
Who o'er a parent's grave
Too late repents,
Too late laments
The bitter pain he gave.

May we ne'er know such grief,
Nor cause one feeling sad;
Let our delight
Be to requite,
And make our parents glad.

CHAPTER II.
THE PRISONER RELEASED.

"Who can say, I have made my heart clean, I am pure from my sin?"—
PROV. xx. 9.

There were many bright young faces in the daily school which was taught by Willy Thorn, but there was one face which, though young, never wore a smile. In play-time many an orange, apple, or cake, was given by the school-boys to each other; but there was one of whom no one ever seemed to think, one who never received even a look of kindness. Many of the boys returned to cheerful homes to repeat to their parents what they had heard from their teacher; but one felt desolate and alone in the world, there was none to welcome him to his wretched dwelling, for such a place cannot be called a home. Why did his companions dislike sitting next in school to the pale boy with the sunken cheek and the drooping eye, and why in the merry hours of play did they seek to exclude him from their circle? Alas! there was a stain on the character of Seth Delmar—he had once been in prison for stealing bread from a baker, he was now shunned and despised as a thief!

The poor boy had deeply repented of his sin, and now bitterly felt its consequences. In vain he showed himself ever ready to oblige, bore meekly the taunts and neglect of his companions, and was most watchful over his own conduct. Thorn remarked the painful position of the child, and feeling that to drive him into despair might be to drive him further into sin, and that not a little self-righteousness was at the bottom of the scorn with which his school-fellows treated the unhappy Seth, he resolved to take the first opportunity of speaking to them upon the subject, and of showing to them their conduct in its true light.

Seth, who was patient and persevering with his tasks, had gained from his teacher the prize of a small book; and the first gleam of pleasure which any one present had ever seen on his wan features, lighted them up for a moment as he received it. It immediately faded away, however, as he glanced timidly round on his companions, and saw that no one cared for his success, that perhaps it would only add to the dislike felt towards him.

The next day Thorn observed the boy bending over this book, while large drops, in spite of his efforts to stop them, forced their way from his eyes as he looked on it. Seeing that something must have occurred, Thorn walked up to the spot, and found out at once the cause of Seth's distress. On the title-page of the book Thorn had written his name; but just under it now appeared, in a very different hand, the single terrible word THIEF!

"This has been a most thoughtless—I wish that I could say only *thoughtless* act," said Thorn, with an expression grave almost to sternness. "I will not ask who is the author of this cruel insult, but we must suppose that he who thus condemns another, notwithstanding the warning, *Judge not, that ye be not judged*, is at least conscious that his own heart is pure, that he never has sinned."

The children looked at each other in silence, and then one of the elder boys, Bat Nayland, muttered, half aloud, "Conscious of never having stolen a farthing!"

"I did not say, conscious of never having *stolen*, but of never having *sinned*. All sin is disobedience to the Most High, as sin to be repented of, and as sin to be punished, whether it be theft, falsehood, or unkindness to another. The law forbidding us to covet in our secret hearts was as solemnly given amid the terrors of Sinai, is as binding upon man as *Thou shalt do no murder*. If the chain-cable upon which the safety of a vessel depends be snapped asunder in a storm, no matter how small be the link that gives way, the chain is as truly broken, and the vessel as certainly in danger, as if it had been dashed into a thousand pieces."

"Still, I do think," said Bat Nayland, "that there are some greater sinners, and greater commandments, and that we are not to be put on a level with thieves."

"Do you remember," said Thorn, mildly, turning to a boy who was near him, "which our blessed Lord Himself said were the two *great commandments* of the law?"

"*Thou shalt love the Lord thy God with all thy heart, and with all thy soul, and with all thy strength. This is the first and great commandment. And the second is like unto it, Thou shalt love thy neighbour as thyself.*"

"And those who break the *great commandments* must, of course, be great sinners?"

There was a general murmur of assent.

"And now tell me," said Thorn, speaking more earnestly, and looking around him as he spoke, "which of us can plead *not guilty* to the charge of having broken these great commandments—broken them often—broken them every day of our lives?"

No voice was raised in reply—conscience was bearing silent witness against all. Thorn continued: "The Almighty has a claim to our greatest love; He has created us, preserved us, redeemed us—He has deigned to say, *My son, give Me thy heart!* but which of us have obeyed the heavenly call? Has it been our delight to serve Him, to pray to Him? have we thought on Him with reverence, gratitude, and love; seeking His glory before our own pleasure, making His will the law of our lives? This it is, my children, to keep the first commandment: if any one present feels in his heart that he never has wilfully broken it, let him now raise up his hand in token that he can say *Not guilty* to this charge!"

Every hand remained motionless and still.

"And who has loved his neighbour as himself? Who has never done an unjust action, nor spoken an ill-natured word, nor harboured an envious thought in his heart? Guilty, all guilty we stand before our God! we have broken His commands, we have offended against His holiness; alas! *who can say, I have made my heart clean, I am pure from my sin*!"

"And now," continued Thorn, after another solemn pause, "which of you here can give me a verse from the Word of God which tells us the just punishment of sin?"

Seth answered, in a very low voice, which would not have been heard but for the great silence which prevailed through the room, "*The soul that sinneth, it shall die!*"

"Then what is to become of us all?" cried William Browne, who had but lately joined the school; "must all be punished, as all have sinned? is there no hope of escape?"

"Our hope is in the blessed Son of God, who came down to earth that He might raise us to heaven—who bore our punishment that we might share His bliss. Through faith in Him even the chief of sinners may be saved—*the blood of Jesus Christ cleanseth from all sin.*"

"But then," said Nayland, "if those who have sinned much, and those who have sinned less, may all go to heaven if they only believe, it seems as if it did not matter whether we tried to obey or not—as though, the Lord having done all, we have nothing left to do."

"God forbid that you should think so," hastily interrupted Thorn. "All must strive for *holiness, without which no man shall see the Lord. If any man have not the Spirit of Christ, he is none of His.* The Bible abounds in passages that show that for the wilfully disobedient, who will not repent, the Lord's despised mercy will but add to the punishment of their sin!"

"I do not quite understand this," said William Browne.

"In order to explain to you how our salvation is only from the Lord, and yet that we must *work out our salvation with fear and trembling*, I will repeat to you a little allegory or parable. Remember that my tale is intended to convey a deeper meaning than what may at first sight appear; exert your minds to discover that meaning, I am telling you the history of man, I am telling you the history of yourselves."

All the school listened with silence and attention, as, after a minute's consideration, the teacher began.

"There was a great and powerful Sovereign, who ruled over an extensive kingdom. But wise and just as were his laws, formed to make all happy who obeyed them, there were rebels who rose against their King, broke his commands, despised his statutes, and most justly deserved the sentence of death pronounced upon them as traitors. Amongst these was a youth, whom I need not name, who, after having had judgment passed upon him, was confined in a prison named *Condemnation*, until the executioner, *Justice*, should be sent to carry out the sentence of the law.

"Very strong was his prison, very thick its walls; the grated window, through which the light scarcely came, forbade all hope of release. Sometimes the youth tried to flatter himself with the idea that his Sovereign was too merciful to destroy him; but then the sentence of the judge rose in his mind, he felt that Justice demanded his punishment. Then he sought amusement to drive away the fear of death, and sometimes succeeded in his miserable efforts to be gay; but still the thought of what was before him forced itself on his mind, and he never could be really happy."

"A wretched state to be in," observed Nayland.

"It is by nature the state of us all," said Thorn. "We have all *sinned and fallen short of the glory of God*; we are all sentenced, and justly sentenced; and but for the hopes of a better life beyond, what would this world be but a prison! But to return to the rebel in my story:—

"One night as, clothed in his dark and ragged attire, he was reflecting upon his unhappy fate, a bright light shone in his prison, and he beheld coming towards him a Friend—one whose kindness he had long neglected, but who had not forgotten him in his adversity. The garments worn by that Friend were white and spotless; there was no stain upon them; they were such as befitted one of high estate, of one of such rank that it might have been little expected that his foot would ever tread the dungeon of Condemnation!

"He addressed the young rebel in terms of love and pity. He told the condemned one that he had quitted everything, risked everything from pure love, to save him from the death which he had deserved. He warned him that Justice was about to enter that prison, to shed the blood of the prisoner within; that there was but one way of escape. If the rebel changed garments with his merciful visitor, put off his own rags to wear that white robe, he might yet make his way from the prison of Condemnation, and pass Justice himself in security! The Friend, moreover, told the rebel that by using the watchword *Faith*, even the guards at the outer door would suffer him to go free; and that he would find outside a guide most trusty and safe, who would lead him to a place of security. Then, as the prisoner, with trembling haste, made the needful exchange of dress, his heart throbbing with the hope of freedom, and, we may also trust, with gratitude to the merciful Being who was content to remain and suffer death in his stead, his Friend placed in his hand a paper, containing his last dying request to the sinner whom he had saved, and charged the youth, if not for his Preserver's sake, yet for his own, to shun for ever those rebels who had led him into the guilt which was now to be atoned for at so fearful a price."

"And did he really escape, and did his merciful Friend really stay and die for him?" cried young Browne.

"You may turn to your Bibles for an answer to that question, and there see who *was wounded for our transgressions* and *bruised for our iniquities*; who came to us when we lay in deep condemnation, and saved us by giving his life for us!"

"I begin to understand your meaning," said Nayland, thoughtfully; "but I never dreamed before that *I was* a rebel, that I was in danger of punishment, or needed such a Friend to suffer what my sins had deserved."

"And the white robe is the garment of the Lord's righteousness?" murmured Seth.

"Yes," said Thorn; "that which we must wear if we would quit the prison, or pass safely the executioner, Justice. And this brings me to the point which I wished to explain, that salvation is *only* from the Lord, and that yet we must *work out our salvation with fear and trembling*. Who can deny that the prisoner owed his escape wholly and entirely to the mercy of his Friend?"

"No one," exclaimed several voices; "he had no power to help himself at all."

"But now, suppose that the prisoner, while yet beneath the shadow of his dungeon, should throw away his disguise as something quite unneeded, should forget his watchword, turn away from his guide, and, notwithstanding the last earnest warning from his Deliverer, hasten to join the rebels again?"

"He would be ungrateful, wicked, mad to do so!" cried the boys; and Nayland added, "He would deserve to be dragged back to his dungeon, and suffer a worse fate than if he never had left it."

"It is so," said Thorn; "and so it will be when the Lord comes to judge the earth. Those who, having tasted of the Saviour's mercy, still persist in joining His foes—who put aside His perfect righteousness, and choose the ways that He has condemned, not repenting of or forsaking those sins which cost His precious life, will be more severely judged than the heathen who have never known Him or His laws."

"There is one thing which I should like to know," lisped the youngest child in the school: "What was put in the paper which the kind Friend gave to the poor prisoner just as he set him free?"

"His dying request, doubtless," said Nayland.

"What words would you say were to be found in that paper?" said Thorn to Edmund Butler, an intelligent boy, who was usually at the head of the school.

Edmund reflected for a moment, and then said, "*If ye love Me, keep My commandments.*"

Thorn saw that an answer was trembling on the lips of poor Seth, and encouraged him by a glance to say it aloud: "*This is My commandment, That ye love one another, as I have loved you.*"

"Here, then," said the teacher, "is the motive of *love.* Remember," he continued, impressively, "that this was our Saviour's dying request, when He who was innocence itself was about to suffer shame, agony, and death for our sakes. Is there one heart here so cold that it would slight the last wish of a dying Friend—so ungrateful that it would seek to make no return for love so exceeding great? Can we think on His mercy, and yet be unmerciful; and, by our unkind, ungenerous conduct towards our fellow-creatures, show that the highest motive has no power over our souls, and that we choose heartlessly and ungratefully to neglect the only way by which we can prove our love to Him who loved us and gave Himself for us?"

There was no immediate answer to this question—perhaps the teacher did not expect to receive one; but as the boys passed out of the school-room, when the lessons were over, Thorn saw with a feeling of pleasure young Nayland walk up to Seth Delmar, and, while his cheek flushed crimson, whisper something in his ear, to which the poor boy replied by warmly grasping his hand. And Seth was no longer persecuted in the school, despised by his companions, or taunted with his sin. The boys had learned to show more indulgence to the failings of others, from having a truer knowledge of their own; and finding that they had all broken the great commandment, and had no hope but from the merits and mercy of their Lord, they looked with more pity upon a poor fellow-sinner, whose transgression had been repented of and forgiven.

No heart is pure from evil; none
Can say before the Holy One,
"I in my strength the race have run,
Have fought the fight successfully!

"In faith and virtue I have dwelt;
No proud, unholy feelings felt,
Nor mocked my Maker when I knelt,
By wandering thoughts of vanity.

"My first desire, in all things seen,
To glorify my God hath been;
My lips are pure, my heart is clean;—
Thou know'st my soul's integrity!"

Ah, no! far other plea be mine,
As at Thy cross, O Lamb divine,
For Thy dear sake, and only Thine,
I ask for mercy tremblingly!

My sins are more than I can count,
Each day is swelling the amount;
All stained with guilt, I seek the Fount
Of holiness and purity.

Forgive the debt that I confess,—
Wash out my sins, my efforts bless;
And clothe me with Thy righteousness,
In time and through eternity!

CHAPTER III.
THE MOTHER'S RETURN.

"Trust in the Lord with all thine heart; and lean not unto thine own understanding."—PROV. iii. 5.

"I am so glad that dear mother is coming back to-day!" cried little Mary Benson; "it seemed as if the week would never be over."

"Yes; if we had not been so busy knitting these cuffs for her, we should have found the time weary indeed," said Maria. "But how much pleased she will be to have them; and what a surprise it will be to her when she did not even know that we could knit!"

"It was very kind in Mrs. Peters to teach us. I hope that she will not let out her secret: mother was to call at her house on her way back, to leave the parcel of wool."

MARIA AND MARY.

"Poor mother! she will be weary enough with her long, tiresome walk."

"She will forget all when she presses us to her heart," cried little Mary, her eyes sparkling with pleasure at the thought. "Oh, to think of being in her dear arms again! How we shall rush into them!"

"If mother could have afforded to pay for the coach, she might have been here by this time; but it seems as if she had never one sixpence to spare," sighed Maria. "I cannot help thinking," added the little girl, after a pause, turning listlessly over the pages of a book which she was rather looking at than reading—"I cannot help thinking that the Almighty cares less for us than He does for the rich and the great. If He is as tender and loving as we are told that He is, how is it that we want for so many things?"

"Oh, Maria, it is very sinful to think in that way! We must trust in the Lord with all our heart; and not, in our naughty pride, fancy that we know what is good for us better than He who is all wisdom as well as love."

"I should like to know why there are such differences in the world," said Maria.

"We must remember what the Saviour said to Peter: *What I do thou knowest not now, but thou shalt know hereafter*. In another world we shall see that all God does is right. Do you not recollect what the clergyman told us in his sermon last Sunday—that if there were no differences of station in this life, the rich would not be able to exercise charity, nor the poor to exercise patience?"

"The task of the rich is much easier than that of the poor," observed Maria, with a discontented look.

"Perhaps not," gently suggested Mary. "I do not think that the Bible makes it appear so: we are so often warned of the dangers of riches; and none of us can tell, if we had them, whether we should make a good use of them. I like those lines which mother taught us to repeat—

'The greatest evil we can fear

Is—to possess our portion here.'"

"We are little likely to suffer from that evil," observed Maria, with a bitter smile. "It does seem to me hard that mother—who is always so religious, and patient, and good—should have to work so hard and yet gain so little, while others have plenty without working at all. It seems as if God were hiding His face from us."

"Oh! *trust in the Lord with all thine heart, and lean not unto thine own understanding*. This is one of the verses which mother told me quiets her mind whenever she is tempted to murmur at her lot. But is not that mother crossing the field? Yes, yes! it is our own dear mother!" And both of the children, with a cry of delight, flew to the door to meet her, carrying their little present in their hands.

WATCHING FOR MOTHER.

But what was the amazement of the girls at the reception which they met with from their mother—from her whom they so tenderly loved and had been so anxiously expecting! Mrs. Benson's face was flushed, her manner hurried. Not one kiss, not one welcome smile, not one kind word did she give; but waving them away impatiently as they sprang forward to welcome her, "Back, back!" she cried; "don't touch me!"—and passing them in a moment, she hastened up-stairs to her own room.

Neither of the children could at first utter a word. With open eyes and lips apart, they stood as if transfixed, their surprise and mortification were so great. Then slowly and sadly they retraced their steps, and returned to the room which they had just quitted. Neither spoke for a little while, till Maria, pettishly flinging down the cuff which she had knitted, exclaimed,—

"Who would ever have thought that mother could be so unkind!"

"Unkind? Oh, never, never say such a word!" cried Mary, her own eyes swimming with tears.

"She looked as if she would have pushed me back—me, her own child!—if I had ventured a little nearer; and after not having seen us for so many days! I cannot think what could make her treat us in such a manner!"

"Don't think, but *trust*," faltered her gentle sister. "We may be certain that mother has good reasons of her own. She always loves us, and acts for our good; and though we cannot just now understand what she does, we may be sure, quite sure, that it is wise and kind."

"Bless you, my child, for your loving trust!" exclaimed her mother, who was at that moment entering the room, and who now pressed her little daughter to her heart more warmly and more tenderly than ever, as though to make up by increasing love for even five minutes' apparent neglect.

"O mother, why would you not let us come near you?" exclaimed Maria, as she, too, shared in the fond embrace.

"For your own sakes, my darlings; only for your own sakes. I had called on Mrs. Peters, as I had promised, on my way; and not till I had entered into her cottage did I know that her only son was then lying there dangerously ill of the scarlet fever."

"Poor Robin!" cried the little girls, full of sympathy for the trouble of their neighbour. "Is not that fever terrible and infectious?"

"Most infectious, my children; and I own that I felt grieved and frightened at having entered the house. I fear not for myself. Were it not for you I should have offered to remain to help to nurse the poor boy: but I dreaded lest I might be carrying here death in my very clothes—that I might be bringing misery into my own happy home; and not till I had laid aside my bonnet and large cloak did I dare to embrace my children. You met me so eagerly at the door that I was obliged to call out very hastily, or you would have been in my arms before I could stop you; and I had no time for explanations then."

"Mother had good reasons," said Maria to herself: "how strange it was that I ever could doubt her!"

"And how is poor Mrs. Peters?" inquired Mary, as her mother took a chair near the fire, and her little daughters seated themselves at her feet. "She is so fond of her son!—she could not live without him. How does she bear this terrible trial?"

"Like a Christian," replied her mother—"like one who knows that all events are in the hands of an all-wise Being, who does not willingly afflict His children. All her hopes and her fears are laid before Him in prayer; and having used all human means to preserve her son, she now rests humbly on the infinite mercy of the Lord, who ordereth all things well. She has been given that trusting, confiding spirit which is so pleasing in the sight of Heaven."

"Ah, that is what I want!" murmured Maria, hiding her head on her parent's knee. "Mother, I have learned a lesson to-day from the pain which it cost me to doubt *your* love, and the shame that I feel now that I ever could have done so. Mary deserved your first kiss, mother. I can love, very greatly love; but she can both love and *trust*."

Trust in the Lord with all thy heart
While sunshine glitters o'er thee;
Oh, choose in youth the better part,
When all is bright before thee!
Nor think thy pleasures will decrease:
'Tis Faith that here brings joy and peace,
And leads to heaven's glory.

Trust in the Lord with all thy heart
When sorrows gather o'er thee;
When lone and desolate thou art,
And all is dark before thee.
'Tis Faith that can the mourner cheer;
'Tis Faith gives hope and patience here,
And leads to heaven's glory.

CHAPTER IV.
THE FRIEND IN NEED.

"Thine own friend, and thy father's friend, forsake not."—PROV. xxvii. 10.

There was not a happier mother in the village than Mrs. Peters, nor a better son than her Robin. She had trained up her child in the way he should go, and it was now his delight to walk in it; she had not shrunk from correcting his faults, and he loved her the better for the correction; she had taught him from the Bible his duty towards his God, and from the same pages he had learned his duty towards his mother. It was a pleasant sight on the Sabbath morning, to see them walking up the little pathway which led to the church—the feeble parent leaning on the strong, healthy son, who carried her Bible and prayer-book for her. Mrs. Peters never had the slightest feeling of envy towards those who appeared above her in the world—she would not have changed places with any one. "They may have riches, fine houses, broad lands," she would say; "but who has a son like mine!"

GOING TO CHURCH.

On the Sunday afternoon, however, Robin did not accompany his mother to church. Perhaps you may suppose that, after his hard work all the week, he thought that he needed a little rest or amusement; that you might have found him at "the idle corner" of the village, joining in the sports of younger companions; and that he considered, like too many, alas! that having given the Sabbath morning to religion, he might do what he pleased with the rest of the day. Let us follow Robin Peters in his Sunday pursuits, and see where, after partaking of dinner with his mother, he bends his willing steps.

ON A VISIT.

Over the common, through the wood, up the steep hill-side! It matters not to him that the way is long; that in winter part of the road scarcely deserves the name of one at all, being almost impassable from slough and snow. Cheerfully he hastens along, with a light springing step; sometimes shortening the way with a hymn, or gazing around on the endless variety of nature, and lifting up his heart to nature's God! There is surely something very pleasant that awaits Robin Peters at the end of his walk, that he always should take it in this one direction; should never give it up, fair weather or foul; and look so happy while pursuing his way!

OLD WILL AYLMER.

He stops at last at the door of a poor little hovel, built partly of mud, and thatched with straw. The broken panes in the single window have been patched with paper by Robin's hand, instead of being, as formerly, stuffed up with rags; but either way they speak of poverty and want. By the miserable little fire—which could scarcely be kept up at all, but for the sticks which Robin has supplied—sits a poor old man, almost bent double by time, the long hair falling on his wrinkled brow, his hand trembling, his eye dim with age. But there is a kindling pleasure even in that dim eye, as he hears a well-known rap at the door; and warm is the press of that thin, trembling hand, as it returns the kindly grasp of Robin!

First there are inquiries for the old man's health, and these take some time to answer; for it is a relief to the suffering to pour out long complaints—it is a comfort to them if one kindly ear will listen with interest and patience. Then the contents of Robin's pockets are emptied upon the broken deal box, which serves at once as chest of drawers and table to the old man, and a seat to the visitors, "few and far between," who find their way to the hovel on the hill. The present brought by the youth varies from week to week. He has little to give, but he always brings something to eke out old Will Aylmer's parish allowance: sometimes it is a little tea from his mother; perhaps a pair of warm socks, knitted by herself; or a part of his own dinner, if he has nothing else to bring to the poor and aged friend of his father.

After the depths of the pockets had been duly explored, Robin, seated on the box, very close to the old man, for Aylmer was extremely hard of hearing, repeated to him, in a loud tone of voice, as much of the morning's sermon as he could remember. He whom age and infirmities kept from the house of God, thus, from the kindness of a youth, every week received some portion of spiritual food. But most did he enjoy when Robin opened the Bible—for, poor as Aylmer was, he was provided with that—and in the same loud, distinct voice read the blessed words which the dim eyes of his friend could no longer see.

After the holy book was closed, it was long before Robin found that he was able to depart, Aylmer liked so much to hear all about his friends and his neighbours—everything which passed in the village in which the old man had once lived. It was something for him to think over during the long, lonely week, to prevent his feeling himself quite shut out from the living world. And Robin had not only to speak, but to listen; and this, notwithstanding the deafness of old Aylmer, was perhaps the harder task of the two. Not only the poor man's sight, but his memory also was failing: his mind was growing weak and childish with age, and his tedious and oft-repeated tales would have wearied out any patience that was not grounded on Christian love! And so the afternoon of the Sabbath passed with Robin Peters, and he returned weary but happy to his home, to enjoy a quiet, holy evening with his mother. He had poured sweetness into a bitter cup; he had followed the footsteps of his compassionate Lord; and he had obeyed the precept given in the Scriptures, *Thine own friend, and thy father's friend, forsake not.*

After what has been written, it is scarcely necessary to add that the life of Robin was a happy one. At peace with God and at peace with man; earning his bread by honest industry; in debt to none, in enmity with none; blessed with friends, cheerful spirits, and excellent health, he was far happier than many who wear a crown. But though religion can support the Lord's people under trials, it does not prevent their having to undergo them like others, and after several years had been spent in comfort and peace, a cloud was gathering over the home of Robin.

One Saturday evening he returned from his work complaining of headache and a pain in his throat. Mrs. Peters concluded that he had taken a chill, and, advising him to go early to rest, prepared for him some simple remedy, which she trusted would "set all to rights." Robin took what she gave him with thanks, but he seemed strangely silent that evening, and sat with his brow resting upon his hand, as though oppressed by a weight in his head. The fond mother grew anxious—who can help being so whose earthly happiness rests upon *one*? She felt her son's hand feverish and hot; she was alarmed by the burning flush on his cheek, and proposed begging the doctor to call. At first Robin objected to this: he had hardly ever known sickness in his life, the medical man lived at some distance, and the night was closing in. In the maladies of the body—but, oh, how much more in those of the soul!—how foolish and dangerous a thing is delay!

Another hour passed, and the fever and pain of the sufferer appeared to increase. Again the mother anxiously proposed to send for the doctor; and this time Robin made no opposition. "Perhaps it might be as well," he faintly said. "I did not like making you uneasy by saying it before—but there has been a case of scarlet fever up at the farm."

The words struck like a knife into the mother's heart! There was not another moment of delay; she hastily ran out to the door of a neighbour, and easily found a friend (for it was often remarked that Mrs. Peters and her son never wanted friends) who would hasten off for the medical man.

Robin in the meantime retired to his bed, feeling unable to sit up longer. The symptoms of his disorder soon became more alarming—a scarlet glow spread over his frame, his pulse beat high, his temples throbbed; and his mother, in an agony of fear which she could only calm by prayer, sat watching for the arrival of the doctor.

Dr. Merton had just sat down to a very late dinner with two old school-fellows of his, whom he had not met for years; and they promised themselves a very pleasant evening together. "Nothing like old friendships, and old friends!" he said gaily, as the covers were removed from the steaming dishes, and they saw before them a comfortable repast, which the late hour and a twenty miles' ride had given all a hearty appetite to enjoy. "Nothing like old friends, old stories, old recollections!—we shall seem to live our school-days over again, and feel ourselves boys once more!"

There was a ring at the door-bell, a very loud ring—there was impatience and haste in the sound of it. "I hope that's nothing to disturb our sociable evening," said Dr. Merton, who, having filled the plates of both his friends, was just placing a slice of roast beef on his own. He paused, with the carving knife and fork still in his hand, as his servant entered the room.

"Please, sir, here's Tom Grange come in haste from Redburn, and he says that Robin Peters is taken very ill, and his mother begs to see you directly."

The knife and fork were laid down, perhaps a little unwillingly, and the doctor arose from his chair.

"Why, Merton, you're not going now!" cried one of his companions.

"Just wait till after dinner," said the other.

"Excuse me; Mrs. Peters is not the woman to send me such a message without sufficient cause. I have known her and her son too for many a long year, and they shall not find me fail them in their trouble."

So the doctor put on his great-coat, took down his hat, begged his friends to do justice to the good cheer provided, and left them, if I must own it, with no small regret, to sally forth in that cold wintry night, tired and hungry as he was. He walked fast, both to save time and to keep himself warm; but his pace would have been even more rapid had he known the agonizing anxiety, increasing every minute, with which his arrival was expected. The door, as he reached it, was opened by the widow, who looked upon him with the breathless earnestness of one who expects to hear a sentence of life or death.

A very short examination of the sufferer enabled the doctor to pronounce that his case was one of decided scarlet fever. Some one must sit up with him and watch him that night; a messenger should instantly be sent with the remedies required; the doctor would himself call the first thing the next morning.

"You do not think my boy—*very* ill, sir?" faltered the mother, folding her hands, and fixing her eyes upon Dr. Merton with an expression of much grief, which touched the kind man to the heart.

"He is ill, I cannot deny that; but keep a good heart, he has youth and a fine constitution in his favour; and I need not remind you, my friend, to apply for help to Him in whose hands are the issues of life and of death."

Oh, how often that night, that long, fearful night, did prayer arise from the widow's low-roofed cottage! It seemed as though the darkness would never be passed. At the end of every weary hour the night-breeze brought the sound of the church-clock to the watcher's ear, while the stars still trembled in the sky. The wick of the candle burned long and low, the last spark in the grate had died out, and there lay the sufferer, so helpless, so still, that it seemed as though his soul were in like manner silently, surely passing from its dwelling of clay!

But with the return of morning's light the fever rose, and the malady took its more terrible form. Robin knew nothing of what was passing around him; even his much-loved mother he recognized no more; his mind became full of strange, wild fancies, the delirious dreams of fever. His mother listened in anguish to his ravings; but a deeper grief was spared her—even when reason no longer guided his lips, those lips uttered not a word that could raise a blush on the cheek of his mother. Robin's conversation had been pure in the days of his health—he had kept his mouth as with a bridle; and the habit of a life was seen even now when he lay at the gates of death! His mother heard his unconscious prayers—words from Scripture instinctively spoken; and while her hot tears gushed more freely forth, she was thankful from the depths of her soul. There was no death-bed repentance here for a life devoted to sin; Robin had not left the work of faith and love for the dregs of age or the languor of a sick-bed. She felt that if Heaven were pleased to take him from her now, *he was safe*, safe in the care of One who loved him better than even she did; though consciousness might never return to him, though he might never again breathe on earth one connected prayer, *he was safe*, in time and in eternity, through the merits of the Saviour whom he had loved.

"O sir! I am so thankful to see you!" exclaimed Mrs. Peters, as, pale and worn with watching, she received the doctor at an early hour of the morning. "My poor boy is very feverish and restless indeed—he does not know me!"—the tears rolled down her cheek as she spoke; "I am scarcely able to make him keep in his bed!"

"You must have assistance," said Dr. Merton, walking up to his patient. Words broke from Robin's lips as he approached him—words rather gasped forth than spoken: "I must go—he expects me; indeed I must go—my own friend and my father's friend." He made an effort to rise, but sank back exhausted on the pillow.

"There is something on his mind," observed the doctor.

"It is that he is accustomed to visit a poor old friend, Will Aylmer, who lives in the hovel on the hill."

"Will Aylmer!" repeated the doctor, as though the name were familiar to him. And well might it be so, for the feeble old man had in years long past served as gardener to his father; and many a time had the little Merton received flowers from his hand, or been carried in his arms, which then were sturdy and strong.

Dr. Merton now examined his patient, and the poor mother read from the doctor's looks, rather than from his words, that he entertained little hope of her son's recovery. As he quitted that home of sorrow, Dr. Merton sighed from mingling feelings.

"I fear that poor Robin is near his last home," thought he; "and yet why should I *fear*, since I believe that for him it will be but an earlier enjoyment of bliss! He has shamed me, that poor peasant boy! Even in his delirium he is thinking of another; he is struggling to rise from the bed of death to go on his wonted visit of kindness to his own and his father's friend! and I, blessed with means so much larger than his, have for thirty long years neglected, nay forgotten, the old faithful servant of my family! I shall look upon poor Will Aylmer as a legacy from Robin. He has done what he could for his friend during life; and by his dying words—if it please God that he should die—he shall have done yet more for the old man."

For three days Robin continued in an alarming state, and his mother never closed an eye in sleep. Love and fear seemed to give her weak frame strength to support any amount of fatigue; or, as she said, it was the goodness of the Almighty that held her up through her bitter trial. On the fourth morning Robin sank into a deep sleep. She gazed on his features, pale and death-like as they were; for the red flush of fever had all passed away, and he lay motionless, silent, but with that peaceful look which often remains when the spirit has departed. A terrible doubt flashed upon the mother's mind, a doubt whether all were not over! She approaches her son with a step noiseless as the dew, the light feather of a bird in her hand. She holds it near to his lips—his breath has moved it!—no! that was but the trembling of her fingers! She lays it on the pillow, her heart throbbing fast—is that the morning breeze that so lightly stirs the down? No; thank God, he still breathes!—he still lives!

Mrs. Peters sank upon her knees, buried her face in her hands, and once more implored Him who had compassion on the desolate widow of Nain, to save her beloved son; "But, O Lord," she added, with an almost bursting heart, "if it be Thy will to remove him to a happier world, give me grace not to murmur beneath the rod, but to say humbly, 'Thy will be done.'"

As she rose from her knees she turned her eyes towards her son, and they met his, calmly, lovingly fixed upon her, with an expression, oh how different from that which they had worn during the feverish excitement of delirium! "You were praying for me," he said, very faintly; "and the Lord has answered your prayer!" The deep joy of that moment would have overpowered the mother, had it not been tempered by a fear that this improvement might be but as the last flash of a dying lamp, and that the danger was not yet over.

But from that hour Robin's recovery rapidly progressed, and the fever never returned. He was weak, indeed, for many a long day; his vigorous arm had lost all its powers—he had to be fed and supported like a child. But it was a delight to Mrs. Peters to do everything for him, and to watch his gradual improvement in strength. Nor, poor as she was, did she ever know want while her son was unable to work. All the neighbourhood seemed pleased to do something for Robin—to help him who had been so ready to help others. The squire's lady sent wine and meat from her own table; the clergyman's wife brought him strong broth; the farmer, his master, supplied him with bacon and eggs; and many a neighbour who had little to give yet joyfully gave of that little.

SEEKING THE LORD.

"How good every one is to me!" exclaimed Robin, as a parcel from the grocer's was opened before him on the first day that he was able to quit his bed. "I only wish that I could send some of this to Will Aylmer; I am afraid that he has missed me while I was ill."

"Oh, he has been looked after," replied Mrs. Peters with a smile: her care-worn face was becoming quite bright again.

"Who has taken care of him?" inquired Robin.

"I must not tell you, my son; you are to hear all from the old man's own lips."

"I am afraid that it will be very long before I am strong enough to visit him;—how glad I shall be to see him again!"

Two or three days after this, a bright warm sun tempted the invalid to take advantage of the doctor's permission, and try a little walk in the open air. Leaning on the arm of his thankful, happy mother, Robin again crossed that threshold which it once seemed so likely that he would only pass in his coffin. It was a sweet morning in the early spring, and oh, how delightful to him who had been confined on the couch of fever was the sunshine that lighted up the face of nature, the sight of the woods with their light mantle of green, the blue sky dappled with fleecy clouds; even the crocus and the snowdrop in his mother's little garden seemed to speak of joy and hope; and pleasant was the feeling of the balmy breeze that played upon his pale, sunken cheek.

"The common air, the earth, the skies,

To him were opening paradise!"

Robin lifted up his heart in silent thanksgiving, and in prayer that the life which the Almighty had preserved might be always devoted to His service.

"Do you feel strong enough, my son, to walk as far as that cottage yonder?" inquired Mrs. Peters.

"I think that, with your arm, I might reach even the tree beyond."

"Then, suppose that we pay a visit to old Aylmer!"

Robin laughed aloud at the idea. "Why, my dear mother, neither you nor I have strength to go one quarter of that distance; I fear that I must delay that visit for some time to come."

"There is nothing like trying," replied Mrs. Peters gaily; and they proceeded a little way together.

"Is it not strange?—I am weary already," said the youth.

"Then we will rest in this cottage for a little."

"It was empty before my illness; if there is any one in it now, a patient just recovered from the scarlet fever might not be made very welcome."

"Oh, you will be made welcome here, I can answer for that," cried Mrs. Peters; and at that moment who should come tottering from the door, joy overspreading his aged face, his eyes glistening with tears of pleasure and affection, but Robin's poor old friend! He grasped the youth's hand in both his own, and blessed God fervently for letting him see the face of his "dear boy" once more!

"But how is this?" exclaimed Robin, with joyful surprise.

The deaf man rather read the question in Robin's eyes than caught the sense of it from words which he scarcely could hear. "Dr. Merton—bless him!—has brought me here, and has promised to care for the poor old man: and he bade me tell you"—Aylmer paused, and pressed his hand upon his wrinkled forehead, for his powers of memory were almost gone—"he bade me tell you that these comforts I owed to you. I can't recollect all that he said, but I know very well that he ended with the words, '*Thine own friend, and thy father's friend, forsake not.*'"

Forsake not thou thy father's friend,

Forsake not thou thine own,

Though care and grief his form may bow,

And frosts of age are on his brow,

And like a leafless willow now

He stands on earth alone.

Forsake not thou thy father's friend,

Revere the hoary head.

Thou mayst have little to bestow

To lessen want or lighten woe,

But who does not the comfort know

Which one kind word can shed!

Forsake not thou thy father's friend,—

So, when thy strength is o'er,

Mayst thou ne'er want a friend in need,

Thy age to cheer, thy footsteps lead;

And He who is "a Friend indeed"

Be thine for evermore!

CHAPTER V.
FORBIDDEN GROUND.

"My son, if sinners entice thee, consent thou not."—PROV. i. 10.

Little Joseph Ashton was idling about the streets of London on a Sunday afternoon. He had been to church in the morning, and had behaved there like a quiet, attentive child: he had brought home the text to his grandmother, and had also learned two other verses from the Bible. Joseph was not without some feeling of religion: in church he often appeared very devout, especially when he heard the sweet music of the hymn. His grandmother found him obedient and loving, and fondly hoped that her dear son might grow up a true servant of the Lord. But, alas! poor Joseph's goodness was often as the morning dew, it could not stand the hot sun of temptation. Like that strange creature called the chameleon, which is said to change its colour according to the objects that are near it, Joseph changed his conduct according to his companions: he had learned many good things both at home and at school, but he had not yet learned to say *No*!

LITTLE JOSEPH.

Little Joseph now stood at the side of the New Road, looking carelessly at the crowds passing before him, watching the tired omnibus horses dragging their heavy loads—alas! that mercy, if not religion, should not give them their one day's rest! There were hawkers, and sellers of sweetmeats behind their tempting stalls, little thinking, poor and often ignorant as they are, that they are doing the work of the Evil One, by leading others to sin! *What shall it profit a man, if he gain the whole world, and lose his own soul? or what shall a man give in exchange for his soul?* What will these poor sinners think of their miserable profits, the heaps of pence collected on the Sabbath, when they stand before the Judge of quick and dead! Oh, for a voice to warn them in time, to persuade them that He in whose hands are all things would abundantly make up to them, here and hereafter, for all that they might give up for His sake; that better, *far better, is poverty than sin*; that it is a happy thing to trust in the mercy of God, who knows and pities their wants; and that *the blessing of the Lord it maketh rich, and He addeth no sorrow thereto.*

I fear that these were not the thoughts of little Joseph, whose mind was just in that vacant state which tempts evil to enter. As he stood with both his hands in his pockets, leaning against an iron lamp-post, two school-fellows of his, Jack and Thomas Higgins, came up to him from behind.

"I say, Joseph," cried Jack, slapping him on the shoulder, "have you any coppers about you?"

"Why, yes; what makes you ask me?"

"I've a mind to some of that pink rock on yon stall—it's the nicest thing in the world. I shared my gingerbread with you yesterday, so it's only fair that you stand treat to-day."

"I'll get some to-morrow," said Joseph, who had a lively remembrance of the impressive manner of the clergyman that morning when he repeated the commandment of the Most High, *Remember the Sabbath-day, to keep it holy.*

THE STREET STALL.

"To-morrow! Oh, nonsense! we want it now."

"You don't mean to say that your old granny has been putting silly fancies into your head about it's being wrong to buy a little barley-sugar on Sunday?" cried Tom, in a mocking tone.

"She'll next say that it's a sin to eat it!" laughed Jack.

Joseph coloured, as though there were anything to be ashamed of in listening to his grandmother, or in obeying his God. He stood fumbling his pence in his pocket, in an uncomfortable, irresolute manner.

"Come, out with it!" cried Jack, "like a good fellow as you are; I'll be bound no one will peach you to your granny."

"I'd not be tied to her apron-strings like a baby!" said Tom. "There! just look at the stall; isn't it tempting?"

Very tempting it certainly was, and poor Joseph was one who had little courage to resist temptation. So he exchanged his pence for the piece of pink rock, which he divided between himself and his companions; who, having obtained all that they wanted from their schoolfellow, sauntered carelessly away.

Joseph was in the act of eating his portion of the sweetmeat, feeling uneasy from a consciousness of doing wrong—for he had not attained that terrible hardness of heart which comes by long practice of sin—when a lady, who took an interest in the school which he attended, approached him on her way towards church. At one glance she recognized the boy, who had been rather a favourite of hers; and his look of shame, yet more than the employment in which he was engaged, and the nearness of the stall at which he had been buying, showed Mrs. Graham that he had been profaning the Sabbath.

"Is any pleasure worth a sin?" she said softly as she passed; and, gently as those words were spoken, they seemed to leave a sting behind. The short enjoyment of the sweetmeat was speedily over; indeed, so unpleasant were the feelings of its purchaser, that it could hardly be said to have been enjoyed at all. Joseph returned home discontented and ashamed; he knew that he had acted both sinfully and weakly, and had neglected the warning in the Bible, *My son, if sinners entice thee, consent thou not.*

A few weeks after this occurrence, Mrs. Graham announced her intention of giving a treat to all the children of the school. She had a pretty country villa but a few miles from town, and invited the scholars to take tea and cake, and spend a half-holiday in her grounds. A large van was hired to convey the whole party; and the expedition to Maythorn Lodge was looked forward to with extreme delight.

A fear certainly crossed the mind of Joseph, that, his late fault having been noticed by the lady, he might be excluded from the treat given to the rest. But it was not so; and when the crowded van drove off, while the merry throng with laughter and shouts clustered within like bees in a swarm, there was none among them gayer or happier than Joseph.

It seemed as if everything combined to heighten the pleasure provided for the children. The weather was neither too hot nor too cold; the delightful sun of May shone to brighten but not to burn; the hedges were gay with the blossoms of spring, and the meadows were spangled with daisies.

Mrs. Graham with cheerful kindness received her young guests. A long deal table had been spread on the lawn; huge piles of sliced cake appeared down the middle; and as the merry, eager children took their places on each side, hot tea was handed round in large kettles. The benevolent lady looked smilingly on, as if sharing the enjoyment which she gave.

THE LAWN.

"And now," said she, when the repast was ended, "I shall leave you to amuse yourselves here. I know that you will enjoy a good merry game, and the lawn will make a capital play-ground. I have but to desire you all to respect my flowers, and, above all, not to run over my strawberry beds; that gravel path shall mark out your bounds—all beyond it is forbidden ground."

A ready promise was instantly made, which, probably, every one intended to keep. The lady thought that there would be little temptation to break it, for the fruit of the strawberry had not yet appeared, though plenty of blossoms on the low green plants gave promise of an abundant supply before long.

For a while no difficulty was felt in obeying the kind lady's command. The flowers were quite safe on their stalks, not a foot touched a strawberry blossom. But, unfortunately, Jack Higgins had brought his bat, and nothing would please either his brother or him but the idea of a game of cricket.

"If we had a field to play in," said Edmund Butler, "there is nothing that I should like better; but there is hardly room for such a game here, for it is very likely indeed that the ball would be sent into the forbidden ground. The strawberry bed would be in danger."

"It certainly would," added Joseph.

"I wish that it stood anywhere but where it does!" exclaimed Tom, preparing two stumps for the wicket; "but I don't believe that we'll do any harm, and I'm quite resolved to have a game!"

There was instantly a division amongst the boys, some deciding to obey the wishes of their kind friend, some to follow their own amusement. I am happy to say that the greater number decided to run no risk of offending her, so that Jack began to fear that he could hardly collect enough of companions to enable him to play at cricket.

"I wonder at you all!" he cried. "It's the manliest game going, and the only one fit for Englishmen! You'll join us, Joe Ashton, I know that you will—there's nobody bowls like you!"

Again the weak boy doubted and hesitated, afraid to do wrong, but without courage to do right. Much rather would he have joined his companions now playing at "hunt the ring;" but the hand of Jack was upon his shoulder; Tom was laughing at his scruples; both urging him to join them; and the struggle ended with him as it usually ended—he could not withstand the persuasion of others.

Joseph was very successful in his bowling; and in the pleasure and excitement of the game thought little of the strawberry bed. As the game proceeded his position in it was changed; he was now one of those who stood to catch the ball, and was eagerly watching the success of his side, ready, like a greyhound, to bound forward if required, when a strong blow from Jack Higgins, who then happened to be batsman, sent the ball right into the midst of the strawberries! Instantly the young player rushed after it: on his quickness the whole game might hang, for the bowler was taking his run. As he reached the ball Joseph's foot tripped, and down he fell, at the very moment when Mrs. Graham and a party of ladies, having come from the house to witness the sports, stood by the edge of the parterre!

"I hope that you have not hurt yourself!" said one of the ladies, as Joseph, flushed and panting, scrambled to his feet.

"He *has* hurt himself," replied Mrs. Graham's displeased voice. Joseph did not venture to lift up his eyes to her face. "He who has disregarded my wishes, and, at the very time when he was experiencing my kindness, wilfully disobeyed my command, has little right to expect more indulgence at my hand. I came prepared with another invitation to the young friends who have visited me to-day. I intended to ask them all to return here again when the summer sun shall have ripened those strawberries, when they shall be welcome to gather them for themselves; but as for Joseph, he has already had more than his share in the blossoms which he has destroyed, which never can bear any fruit—there is no use in his coming to look on while others enjoy what might have been his, if he could have learned the duty of obedience!"

Then was the time for Jack and Tom to have stepped forward and honestly owned their share in the fault. But I appeal to those who, like Joseph, have weakly yielded to the persuasions of those who tempted them to do wrong, whether the companions who have led them into trouble are the ones to try to help them out of it. The Higgins both were silent, and for this time escaped the punishment which is certain, sooner or later, to overtake those who persevere in a course of rebellion. Joseph's heart swelled, a choking feeling was in his throat: to be thus disgraced before all, and debarred from a treat which he would so greatly have enjoyed, and to know that the punishment was just, turned all the pleasure of the day into bitterness.

Mrs. Graham saw his look of distress, and her gentle heart pitied the boy, though she felt too strongly how important the lesson might be to him through the whole course of his future life, to relax in her firm resolve. She followed him, however, as he sadly walked away to a more retired part of the garden. She laid her hand on his arm: he started, for he had not heard her noiseless step as she approached.

"You are very sorry for what has happened, Joseph—I see that you are; you are very sorry to have displeased a friend and forfeited a pleasure."

Joseph looked fixedly on the ground, while his eyes gradually filled with tears. "They made me do it!" at last he muttered, in a low tone. Without appearing to notice the interruption, the lady proceeded: "I should have willingly overlooked your fault, had it been the first brought under my observation; but it is not long since I had reason to believe you guilty of a much more serious offence. You have now only disobeyed an earthly friend—you had then broken the solemn law of your God. You have deprived yourself now of a little pleasure; but who can say how great will be the loss, both in this world and in the next, of him who wilfully profanes the holy Sabbath of the Lord, the maker of heaven and earth!"

MRS. GRAHAM AND JOSEPH.

"They made me do it!" again murmured the boy.

"Heaven forgive them for tempting a weak brother; but their fault does not justify you. What would you say of the soldier who could be persuaded to go over to the side of the enemy? or the subject who, from fear of a laugh or a jest, could desert the cause of his king? Ask strength from the Lord to stand firm in the right, though you alone should defend it: fear nothing but the displeasure of a holy God. Keep his Sabbaths unbroken, and rest assured that you shall find them yield rich fruits of peace and of joy. Oh, *follow not the multitude to do evil. When sinners entice, consent thou not.* They may laugh down your doubts and your scruples now, but they cannot excuse your sin, nor save you from its punishment in the terrible day of judgment."

When sinners entice,
And from thee would wrest
That gem beyond price,
The day God hath blest.
The day that was given
Our souls to prepare
For the sabbath of heaven—
Oh, shun thou the snare!

When fools treat with scorn
What God hath approved,
Their laugh must be borne,
Thy faith be unmoved.
As arrows fall lightly
On mail-covered breast,
The soul that acts rightly
Need ne'er fear the jest.

Oh! follow not thou
The crowd to do ill;
What many allow
May be perilous still.
The sins of another
Excuse not thine own;

The fall of a brother
Is warning alone.

Though hand joined in hand,
The Scriptures will tell,
How on a whole land
Dread punishment fell;—
The flames of Gomorrah,
The waves of the Flood,
Bereaved Egypt's sorrow,
And Palestine's blood!

"When sinners entice,
Consent not, my son;"
Paths many has vice—
Salvation but *one*:
The Christian's allegiance
By faith he must prove—
Faith working obedience—
The obedience of love!

CHAPTER VI.
CLOUDS AND SUNSHINE.

"The hope of the righteous shall be gladness."—PROV. x. 28.

"It will rain, I tell you!—it will rain!" cried Priscilla; "it always does when one wishes it to be fine! So you need not put on your bonnet, Lucy; there will be no boating for us to-day."

"It is not raining one drop—the grass is quite dry," replied Lucy, running for the twentieth time to the door.

"But the sea-weed that hangs there is quite soft and damp, and that is a sure sign of rain. Only see these black, heavy clouds!"

"Only see that dear little bit of bright blue between them! I think, Priscilla, that you are always looking out for clouds. I never notice them at all till the rain begins to drop!"

"That is because you are a thoughtless, foolish little thing!" observed her sister, with a kind of scornful pity.

"Well, I'm glad that I'm not so wise as you; I'd rather be merry than wise," was the laughing Lucy's reply.

This time, however, it appeared that the elder sister was the mistaken one. The patch of blue in the sky, to Lucy's delight, became larger and larger; the sun shone out cheerfully; and, no longer afraid of the weather, both girls set out on their walk towards Ryde. They were there to meet their uncle, a boatman, who had promised them a row over the water to Portsmouth, where he was to show them the docks and feast them with cakes; and as the girls had never been to England before, having been both born and brought up in the Isle of Wight, they had both looked forward to this expedition for a very long time, though with different feelings, according to their different dispositions. Lucy was all delight at the thought of the pleasure—Priscilla all fear lest anything should occur to prevent their being able to enjoy it.

They made their way over the fields—the one mirthful, the other grave. They shortened part of the distance by passing along a lane; and a lovely lane it was, all adorned with wild-flowers.

"I like this path so much!" cried the happy little Lucy. "Such beautiful plants grow in the hedges, that, were I not in a very great hurry to get on, I should gather a splendid nosegay on the way!"

LUCY AND PRISCILLA.

"I do not like this path at all," replied her elder sister; "it is so narrow, one is caught every minute by the thorns."

"Ah, Priscilla! you are always looking out for thorns! I never think of them till I find myself caught."

"That is because you are a silly, giddy child!" was Priscilla's contemptuous reply.

It will be easily seen, from this short conversation, that however wise Priscilla might be in the eyes of other people, or in her own, she was not the most pleasant companion in the world. She was considered a very sensible girl, one possessing reflection beyond her years; and in some respects she deserved the character. She was wise in keeping clear of evil society; she was wise in performing her daily duties, and in not expecting too much from the world: but she was *not* wise in ever casting a shade of gloom over what Providence intended to be bright; she was *not* wise in ever meeting misfortune half-way—in always looking at the dark side of every event, and seeming as though she thought it almost a sin to be happy! In truth, in these matters, by taking the opposite extreme, Priscilla was just as foolish as her sister. The one, eager after pleasure, often met with disappointment: the other, fearing disappointment, scarce knew pleasure at all.

There was the same difference between them on the subject of religion, in which both had been carefully instructed. Lucy was too easily carried away by amusement: with a warm heart, but a giddy and thoughtless spirit, she too often, alas! neglected the *one thing needful* for the passing diversion of the hour. Priscilla never forgot her Bible reading or her prayer; but both were too often a mere matter of form. She would not for any temptation have worked, bought or sold, on the Sabbath; but she never considered it a delight. Priscilla quite put aside the commandment in the Bible, *Rejoice evermore; and again I say unto you, Rejoice*; while her sister forgot, in her heedless mirth, that it is also written, *Rejoice with trembling*. The one girl knew too little of *the fear of the Lord*; the other was a stranger to his *love*.

At length the sisters reached the shore, and saw before them the sparkling waves of the sea. On the waters large men-of-war were lying at anchor; little boats were floating on the sunny tide; some moving on steadily, as their line of oars rose and fell; others speeding along with graceful motion, like butterflies spreading their silver wings. Amongst the many boats which were plying here and there, and those which were fastened to the pier, Priscilla and Lucy vainly searched for the *Nautilus*, which was that which belonged to their uncle. As with anxious looks they proceeded along the shore, exclamations of impatience bursting from their lips, they were approached by an old friend of their uncle's, whom they had seen several times before.

"On the look-out, eh?" said the old sailor, as he came towards them. "You'll not hail the *Nautilus* to-day. Your uncle was engaged this morning by a gentleman to carry him round to the Undercliff in his boat; and I suspect that they'll have ugly weather," he added, turning his weather-beaten face towards the sea, "so he asked me to wait for you here, and tell you why he could not give you a row over the water; and, as he thought as how you might be a little disappointed, he sends you a shilling a-piece to make all straight."

Tears burst from the eyes of little Lucy: she turned aside that the sailor might not see them. Delighted as she ever was at the prospect of pleasure, she never could bear to lose it; and every little disappointment appeared to her as a real and serious misfortune. Priscilla showed less vexation at losing her excursion, though she took the shilling with a discontented air; and her first words, as she turned to walk back with her sister, were as unjust as they were ungrateful to that good Providence that gives us so much even upon earth to enjoy.

"I knew that it would be so! it always happens thus! If one expects a little pleasure, disappointment is sure to come!"

"How strange and unkind in my uncle!" said Lucy, still half crying; "and to think that these stupid shillings could make up for the loss of such a delightful treat!"

"We had better walk faster," observed her prudent sister; "your blue bit of sky is quite disappearing now."

"And these thorns are very annoying," Lucy added, fretfully, as, trying too hastily to free herself from a bramble, she tore a large hole in her dress.

"Life seems all full of clouds and of thorns," observed Priscilla, in the tone of one who is conscious of uttering a very wise saying; "and to hope to find it anything else is folly only fit for a very little child. There!—was not that a drop of rain? Yes; another and another, and so large! That great cloud is going to burst just over our heads, and, as always happens, them is no place near where we could take shelter from a storm."

"Oh, you are wrong there for once! there is Bertha Fielding's cottage; it is a little, a very little out of our way, and I am sure that the good woman will make us welcome."

Thither ran the two little girls in the rain, which was now falling thick and fast. A sudden flash of lightning quickened their steps, till, heated and breathless, they slackened their pace as they approached the neat little cot. There was the voice of a woman singing within—a feeble, trembling voice, in which little melody was left; but its tones sounded earnest, as if coming from the heart, and from a heart that was cheerful and happy,—

"Content with this, I ask no more,

But to Thy care the rest resign;

Sick or in health, or rich or poor,

All shall be well if Thou art mine!"

The girls' hasty tap silenced the hymn, and a kind voice bade them come in. The inside of the cottage was clean and neat, but its appearance bespoke great poverty. The clock, which had once merrily ticked on the whitewashed wall, was gone from its place; there was no arm-chair by the side of the fire; and many a treasured family piece of old china had disappeared from the wooden shelf. A pale, sickly-looking woman lay upon the bed, which was now almost the sole furniture of the little abode. Her countenance appeared worn with pain and with want; yet it still bore a peaceful, hopeful expression.

"May we wait here a little, till the shower is over?" said Priscilla, as she entered the cottage.

"Most heartily welcome," replied Bertha. "I was rather inclined just now to feel sorry at the rain falling, as I suffer a good deal from the damp; but I was wrong, for it has brought me two visitors to-day, and that is a real pleasure in this lonely place."

"I am afraid that you are very poorly," said Lucy, approaching her kindly.

"I am quite laid up at present with rheumatism, my dear, and have been so for the last six weeks. I can scarcely rise from my bed."

"What a misery to have to lie so long on your bed!" cried Priscilla, who had known something of illness.

"What a mercy to have a good bed to lie on!" replied the sufferer, with a patient smile.

"But you will recover before long, and be able to work again," said Lucy, with kind interest in her looks.

"I hope so, if it please God," answered Bertha.

"Ah!" cried Priscilla, "I daresay that you have been hoping and hoping all the time that you have been ill."

"I always cherish hope, my dear."

"Then you are disappointed every day of your life."

"Oh no!" cried the sick woman, cheerfully; "my hope is firm and sure, and can never be disappointed."

"That is impossible," said Priscilla.

"Oh, tell me your secret!" cried Lucy, with animation. "I always am hoping too, but I so often find that I never can have what I hope for."

"My secret is a very simple one," replied Bertha. "I ask the Lord, for the sake of His blessed Son, to give me all that is good for me; and I hope—I more than *hope*—I feel *certain*—that the Lord hears and will grant my prayer."

"Yet you are sent poverty and pain," said Priscilla.

"I firmly believe that both poverty and pain will work together for my good, and that I shall suffer from neither of them one moment longer than the all-wise Father knows to be best for His child."

"Yet you must be very miserable now," said Priscilla, glancing round on the almost comfortless abode, and then at its suffering inmate.

"Miserable! oh no; that is no word for a Christian! When I think of my deserts, and then of all that is left me, I should think it a *sin* to be miserable."

"A sin!" repeated Priscilla, in surprise; "and what have you to make you anything else?"

"Some comforts even of this earth. I have never yet gone one day quite without food; God has till now provided me with daily bread. I have a roof over my head, and some kind friends, and one friend"—here she laid her hand on a Bible—"that casts sunshine over the darkest trial. My hearing and my eyesight are spared to me—how great a blessing is this! Then I have sweet thoughts to cheer me as I lie here in pain. I trust that, through my Saviour, my sins have been forgiven. Is that no cause for happiness? I trust that every hour brings me nearer to a home where there shall be no more sorrow, or crying, or pain. Is that no cause for happiness? I believe that my gracious God is with me even here, to support my courage and keep me from falling. Is that no cause for happiness? Oh, well may I count up my mercies! well may I thank Him who bestowed them all!—the Rock of my strength and my salvation!" Tears filled her eyes as she spoke, but not tears of sorrow: *The hope of the righteous shall be gladness.*

Priscilla sighed. When she contrasted her lot with that of this poor woman—her peevish discontent, her cold, heartless service, with Bertha's loving, grateful, happy spirit—she felt abashed and humbled in her own eyes.

"The rain is over," she said, turning to the door. "I am sure that we are much obliged to you, Bertha; and I shall often think over what you have said."

Lucy glided to her sister, and whispered a few words to her, at the same time pressing something into her hand. "You speak for me," was all that could be overheard. Priscilla's smile was brighter than usual.

"We happen to have been given a little money," she said, going up to Bertha with Lucy; "we have no real wants ourselves, and we should be glad, very glad, if you would spend it in getting any little comfort for yourself."

"May the Almighty bless you for your kindness, dear children!" cried Bertha, fervently clasping her hands. "It is He who has sent you here to-day. He knew that I had not a crust left in my cottage—that I had no earthly means of procuring one. He has answered my prayer. I hoped in Him, and He has not disappointed my hope. But I cannot deprive you of both shillings," she added; "it is too much—"

"Oh no!" exclaimed Priscilla; "we will never touch that money again!"

"Prissy," said Lucy gaily to her sister, as they hastened along the wet path, not complaining when their shoes were fixed in the mire, and showers of moisture dropped on them from the trees, "I am almost glad now that we were disappointed of our treat; I think that it was a good thing after all."

"Yes; and I am glad that the shower came, though we dreaded it so much."

"I daresay that if we looked at things as poor Bertha looks, we should find a great deal to make us glad."

"Glad, and thankful besides," said Priscilla.

"Ah, you are thinking less of the thorns and the clouds!"

"I see that earthly joys and earthly sorrows are mixed, like the lovely wild-flowers with the brambles; so that we should not care too much for the one, nor fret too much at the other. And as, when dark clouds roll over the sky, we yet know that the blue heaven is always beyond, we may look through all troubles with a sure glad hope."

"*And the hope of the righteous shall be gladness*," said Lucy.

Oh! who should be joyful and glad,

If not those whom the Saviour has loved,

Who, living or dying, their happiness rest

On the Rock which can never be moved?

What have we, as sinners, deserved?

What hath God in His graciousness given?

Let us love Him and serve Him, rejoicing below,

As we hope to do always in heaven.

Can myriads of glittering lights

E'er equal the brightness of day?

Or all that the world holds of pleasure and wealth
The joys of religion outweigh?
What have we, as sinners, deserved?
What hath God in His graciousness given?
Let us love Him and serve Him, rejoicing below,
As we hope to do always in heaven.

Shall we murmur at pains or at grief,
If our God be our Father and Friend?
Those pains—they can bring us but nearer to Him;
That grief—oh, how soon it will end!
What have we, as sinners, deserved?
What hath God in His graciousness given?
Let us love Him and serve Him, rejoicing below,
As we hope to do always in heaven.

CHAPTER VII.
THE GREAT PLAGUE.

"Fools make a mock at sin."—PROV. xiv. 9.

"What a violent storm is raging!" said Thorn the teacher to his scholars, as, after having dismissed them at the close of the school hours, he found them clustering together in the porch, afraid of venturing forth into the pelting rain, pouring down in large, heavy drops, mingled with hail, which danced on the wet, brown pavement. "Come back into the room, my children: it is better than standing there in the cold. Amuse yourselves as you like until the weather clears up, while I occupy myself with reading."

The boys gladly availed themselves of the permission, and began to play together in one part of the room, while the weary teacher sat down in another, rested his pale brow on his hand, and tried, as far as the noise and talking would let him, to forget his fatigue in a book.

He soon, however, found it impossible not to hear what was passing; his eye rested, indeed, on the page, but his mind could not take in the sense of it. He loved his pupils too well to think that his care of them should end with the hours of study: he looked on the immortal beings committed to his charge as those for whom he must one day render an account to his God and theirs.

"No, we're all tired of that!" cried the voice of Bat Nayland, as some well-known game was proposed. "I know something that will give us a deal more fun: let's play at the highwayman and the judge!"

"What's that? what's that?" cried a dozen young voices.

"Oh! it's what I saw at the penny theatre, about a clever thief robbing a judge: only think—robbing a judge!" The last words were repeated around the room in various tones of amusement and surprise.

"Oh! you shall know all about it: but first we must arrange the parts. You, Pat, shall be the thief, and I will be the judge—no, you shall be the judge and I the thief!" He was interrupted by a burst of laughter.

"Be quiet, will you?—who'll be the policeman?"

"I! I!" cried several of the children, eager to join in the proposed play.

"Now, Sam, you shall be the fat landlady,"—there was another roar of merriment, louder than before;—"for you must know that the thief is to get drunk; that's how he is to be taken by the policeman; and he staggers here and there,"—Bat began to imitate the unsteady movements of an intoxicated man, amid the renewed mirth of the children;—"and when they seize him he calls out a great oath—you shall hear it all just as I heard it."

"I hope not," said Thorn, very quietly, raising his eyes from his book. The boys were quiet in a moment: they had almost forgotten the presence of their teacher.

"Why, sir, do you think that there is any harm?" said Bat Nayland: "it does not make us thieves to have a little fun about them."

"It lessens your horror for their crime; and remember the words in the Bible, *Fools make a mock at sin.* Can you imagine any true child of God laughing at theft, drunkenness, and swearing?"

There was profound silence in the room.

"This is one cause, I believe, why penny theatres are one of the most fruitful sources of vice and ruin to those who attend them. Wickedness, instead of appearing hateful as it does in God's Word, is made amusing, and even sometimes attractive; and those who willingly place themselves in the way of being corrupted by such sights, only mock the Holy One when they pray, *Lead us not into temptation.*

THE TEACHER'S STORY.

"But," continued the teacher in a more cheerful tone, "if I have stopped your amusement in one way, it is but fair that I should contribute to it in another. I hear the rain still pattering without—what would you say to my telling you a story?"

"A story! a story!" repeated the scholars, forming in a little circle around their teacher; for where are the children to be found upon earth on whom that word does not act like a spell!

"It is now long, long ago," commenced Thorn, "nearly two hundred years, since the fearful plague raged in London. Nothing which we have witnessed in these happier days can give an idea of the horrors of that time. It is said that nearly seventy thousand people perished of this awful malady—some authors make the number even ninety thousand! The nearest relatives were afraid of each other. When an unfortunate being showed symptoms that the disease had seized him—the swelling under the arms, the pain in the throat, the black spots, which were signs of the plague—his very servants fled from him in terror; and unless some one was found to help the sufferer from love even stronger than fear of death, he was left to perish alone; for the plague was fearfully infectious. When a door was marked with a cross, the sign that the fearful scourge had entered the house, it was shunned by all but the driver of the dead-cart—that gloomy conveyance which moved slowly through the silent streets to carry away the bodies of those who had sunk beneath the terrible disease!"

"Was London ever in such a horrible state?" cried Bat Nayland; "it must have been a thousand times worse than the cholera!"

THE PLAGUE IN LONDON.

"What I have told you about it I believe to be strictly true; I leave you all, however, to judge whether what I am about to relate can be so.

"In a small house, at the time when the plague was raging, dwelt a widow with five young children. She loved them with the fondest, truest love: they were all that were left her in the world. From the first appearance of the plague in London her heart had been full of painful anxiety—far less for herself than for them. Determined to take every human precaution to guard her little ones from danger, she forbade them to quit the house, which she only left herself in order to procure food, holding a handkerchief steeped in vinegar before her face, as far as possible to keep out infection. Her anxiety became yet more distressing when she saw one morning on the door of the very opposite house the fatal sign marked, and below it chalked the heart-touching words, 'Lord have mercy upon us!'

"That day the mother was compelled to go out for bread. She left her home with a very heavy heart, first looking earnestly upon all and each of her children, to see if they yet appeared healthy and well, repeating her command that none should stir out, and inwardly breathing a prayer that the Almighty would preserve them during her absence.

"As she returned with hurried steps towards her home, shuddering at the recollection of the sights of horror which she had seen in the course of her walk, with terror she observed her eldest son *playing upon the very threshold of the infected house*, and trying to imitate with a piece of chalk the dreadful signs upon the door!"

"The little idiot!"—"He must have been without his senses!"—"What did the poor mother do?" were the exclamations which burst from Thorn's listeners.

"She could not speak, in the transport of her anger and grief: she seized him by the arm, and dragged him into her own house, with feelings which only a mother can understand. She found her four other children assembled in her little parlour, amusing themselves by—would you believe it?—playing at *catching the plague*!"

"Oh no, no!" cried the children at once. "You told us that we should judge whether the story were true, and we are sure that this cannot be true!"

"And why not?" inquired the teacher.

"Because," answered Bat, replying for the rest, "the plague was too horrible a thing to make a joke of! Just at a time when their mother was so anxious, when thousands were suffering so much around them—no, no! that would have been too bad; they could never have made game of the plague!"

"And yet what were my pupils doing ten minutes ago but making game of a far worse disease than the plague—the fatal disease of sin? Its spots are blacker, the pain it gives more terrible: often has it caused the death of the body, and, except where repented of and forsaken, the death, the endless death of the soul! Oh, my children! it may be your lot, as it was that mother's, to be *obliged* to go out and meet the danger, for the Almighty may have seen good to place you in situations of great temptation; but if so, take every means of guarding your own hearts, by faith, watchfulness, and prayer. But oh, never wilfully throw yourselves into temptation—*do not play upon the threshold of the infected house*—do not trifle with the danger which it is possible to avoid: and when inclined to think lightly or speak lightly of that which brought ruin and death into the world, remember that *fools make a mock at sin*, but that to free us from its terrible disease, and the fatal consequences which it brings, cost the Eternal Son of the Most High tears, blood, and even life itself!"

Fools make a mock at sin; but oh,

God's wiser children do not so:

They know too well the strife with sin,

How hard the battle is to win;

They laugh not at the wound within,

For they its danger know.

Oh, guide thy mirth by wisdom's rules,

For sorrow ends the laugh of fools!

Fools make a mock at sin; but oh,

Lost, guilty spirits do not so:

They know too well the price it cost;

They know through it that heaven was lost.

No drowning seaman, tempest-tost,

Jests as he sinks below!

Oh, guide thy mirth by wisdom's rules,

For sorrow ends the laugh of fools!

Fools make a mock at sin; but oh,

God's holy angels do not so:

For they upon the Cross have gazed,—

The Cross which sin, *our* sin, had raised,—

And viewed all wondering and amazed,

A Saviour's life-blood flow!

Then write these words thy heart within,—

Fools, and fools only, mock at sin!

CHAPTER VIII.
THE GREEN VELVET DRESS.

"Better is a dinner of herbs where love is, than a stalled ox and hatred therewith."—PROV. xv. 17.

"Wrap your cloak tight round you, my lass; for the wind's bitter cold this morning: and here—see—you wouldn't be the worse of my bit of a shawl under it."

"Oh but, mother, remember your rheumatics."

"I'm a'most right again, Jenny, and I ben't out in the cold," said the poor woman, stirring the few glowing embers which scarcely gave even the appearance of a fire.

"And come back soon again, Jenny dear," cried a pale, bare-footed little boy, running from the corner; "I hope the grand lady won't keep you long."

"I must seek for early violets in the hedges for you, Tommy."

"No, I don't want the violets, I want you back;" and the little thin arms were thrown round her neck, and the child's lips pressed to her cheek.

"O Tommy! I wish I were a grand lady!—I wish I had plenty of money! Shouldn't you have meat enough, and all kinds of food, to make you strong and hearty again!"

"And new shoes!" suggested the child.

"And a blazing fire, and—"

"Hush, my children!" said the mother gently, "and don't let your thoughts go running after what God Almighty has not seen good to give us. We've a-many blessings in this little cot of ours, and I always say that the three prime ones, sunshine for the eyes, hope for the heart, and love in the home, are as free to the poor as to the rich."

The sharp, cutting cold of a March wind, which drove the icy sleet against her face, did not tend to make little Jenny share her mother's spirit of contentment. She hastened up the long hill, holding her bonnet to keep it on, and wishing that she had some better protection against the blast than her thin cloak or her mother's thread-bare shawl. She was to call at the house of a milliner, for whom she was accustomed to run errands and to do little pieces of plain work, in order to carry a parcel from her to a lady who lived at the Hall about three miles distant.

JENNY IN THE STORM.

Jenny arrived at the milliner's, her cheeks glowing with exercise and the cold.

"Take a seat by the fire, and warm yourself, Jenny; I've just a stitch more to put to this trimming, and the dress will be ready for you to take to Lady Grange in two minutes."

So Jenny sat down and looked on with admiring eyes, as the finishing touch was given to a dress which, to her, appeared the very perfection of beauty and splendour.

"It must be a pleasure," thought the girl, "even to touch that lovely soft green velvet; and what must it be to wear it! I could not fancy any one's ever feeling unhappy in such a dress!"

It was a very foolish thought certainly; but I have known people older than Jenny Green who have made reflections just as foolish. Those who suffer from the pressure of poverty are apt to forget that there are other and worse evils in the world; and that just as heavy a heart may, and often does, beat under a robe of velvet as beneath a thread-bare cloak.

The dress was finished, folded, wrapped up in linen, and confided to the girl, with many an injunction to carry it carefully, and not to loiter on the way; injunctions which Jenny conscientiously obeyed, being duly impressed with the importance of her errand, and the amount of confidence reposed in her. The size of her parcel occasioned her some inconvenience: she had no longer a hand free to hold on her bonnet, which, blown back on her shoulders, only hung by its faded ribands, while the gale made sad untidy work with her hair. Jenny's shoes were very old, and the road steep and stony—she became both foot-sore and tired; but her worst trouble was the uneasy, discontented thoughts, which seemed to flow into her bosom from the parcel which she carried.

THE MESSAGE.

"How nice and warm and comfortable it feels! I don't believe that the lady who will wear it ever knows what it is to be hungry or cold. She is never tired, for she has a fine coach to ride in—oh! how grand it must be to ride in a coach! And then to dress like a queen, and feast on good things every day! How very, very happy she must be! I wish that I were a lady, that I do! I'd have a velvet dress of a different colour for every day in the week; and dear Tommy should have a white pony to ride on; and mother, oh! darling mother! should have everything nice that I could think of—she should never have time to wish for anything: how happy we should all be together! But there's no use thinking about it," added Jenny sadly, as on the crest of the hill a sudden gust of wind almost carried her off her feet; "I shall never be rich, nor a lady; I shall have to work and to want all my life through."

The road now led down into the valley, where the way was comparatively sheltered. Jenny felt this to be a pleasant change, though the view was not so grand or extensive as it appeared from the higher ground. She was not, however, enough of a philosopher to remark, even had she known enough of the world to perceive, that in life, as in nature, some of the sharpest blasts are felt by those who *stand on the top of the hill.*

Jenny arrived at length at the grand outer gate, and passed with a timid step through the park, where the tall trees yet stretched leafless branches, though the tiny wild-flowers at their feet were already opening their blossoms to the spring. There was a beautiful garden in front of the house; and along its smooth gravel walks, wrapped up in velvet and furs, sauntered the lady who was mistress of the place.

She stopped to speak to the little messenger. Her manner was gracious and gentle; but Jenny could not help noticing how mournful was its tone; and when she ventured to raise her eyes to the face of the lady, she saw on it an expression of melancholy and care, which raised a feeling of pity as well as of surprise. Is it upon the brow of the poor alone that we see the deep lines of sorrow? is it the cheek of the poor alone that is furrowed by tears? Are the merriest faces those that look from carriage windows? can wealth shut out sorrow, sickness, bereavement, disunion, or death?

Lady Grange noticed the tired looks of Jenny, and kindly ordered the maid whom she had summoned to receive the dress, to take the girl to the kitchen, that she might have a little rest and refreshment. As Jenny, after dropping a courtesy, turned to follow the servant, her attention was arrested by the sudden clatter of horses' feet; and three young men, laughing and racing each other up the slope, dashed along to the entrance of the Hall, the hoofs tearing up the well-rolled gravel, and the loud merry voices strangely breaking the peaceful silence which had prevailed a few minutes before. Two of the horsemen reined up at a little distance from the lady; while the third, who was mounted on a splendid white horse, approached the spot where she stood.

"Mother," said he, stroking the neck of his steed, which champed its bit and pawed on the ground, as if impatient to bound onward again; "mother, I've asked Jones and Wildrake to stop dinner to-day."

Jenny happened to glance at Lady Grange. There was an anxious frown on the gentle face, a flush on the lately pale cheek, which gave an impression of keen suffering not unmixed with anger. What Lady Grange replied to her son, or whether she replied at all, Jenny did not know; for the lady's-maid led her towards the kitchen.

The delicious, savoury odour of that place; the ranges of tin pans on the shelves glittering like silver; the rows of innumerable plates and dishes—above all, the enormous joint, slowly revolving before a fire larger than any that Jenny had ever dreamed of, for the moment put everything out of her head but the thought that it must be delightful to be very rich! "How proud one would be, too, to have so many servants, some of them looking themselves so very grand!" thought Jenny, as she saw various members of the household, some engaged in different occupations, some appearing as though they had nothing to do but to loiter about and gossip. An aged woman, in black bonnet and shawl, was seated at the long deal table on which the stout cook was rolling out some tempting-looking pastry. She, as Jenny soon found from the conversation going on around her, was Mrs. Dale, a nurse who had attended Lady Grange in her childhood, and who had now come from some distance on a visit to that lady, whom she had not seen since her marriage.

"Well, only think!" cried the lady's-maid who had conducted Jenny into the kitchen; "only think! here's Master Philip has brought down those two companions of his whom missus cannot abide the sight of; and they're to stay dinner, and sleep here too, I'll warrant you! I wonder what master will say to it when he comes home."

"Mighty little peace there'll be in the house," observed the cook.

"Oh! as for peace, no one looks for it in this place!" observed the butler, who, with his hands behind him, was warming himself at the fire. "If you'd heard all I've heard, and seen all I've seen!" and he shook his head with an air of much meaning.

"I'm afraid my poor lady has not much comfort in her son?" said the nurse, in a tone of inquiry.

"Comfort! well, I can only say that high tempers and high words—one pulling one way, and another another—the father trying to bridle the son, the son kicking against the authority of the father—debts to be paid, bills to be discharged—Sir Gilbert choosing to do neither, yet having at last to do both—are not my notion of comfort!"

"Master Philip will break his mother's heart," said the lady's-maid;—"you should see how she cries her eyes out when she's in her own room!"

"Master Philip's not such a bad fellow, after all," remarked the butler; "he'd have done well enough if he hadn't had the ill luck to be born heir to a large fortune!"

"Oh! he was spoilt from a baby!" cried the cook.

"'Tisn't so much that," said the moralizing butler, seating himself by the fire and leaning back on his chair. Jenny, who, while taking the cold meat with which she had been provided, could not avoid hearing what was passing, listened with wonder to the easy, and, as it seemed to her, the insolent manner in which the affairs of the Hall were discussed in the kitchen. She began quite to change her mind as to the advantage of keeping many servants; her simple, honest heart, revolted from the treachery of their gossiping with any stranger about the most private concerns of the family which they served. "I'm glad we've our own little cot to ourselves," was the thought which crossed Jenny's mind; "and that we have not a set of people about us to watch every look, listen to every word, and make our troubles known to all the world!"

"You see," continued the butler, addressing himself to Mrs. Dale, "here's the mischief of the thing: Young master found out that he was a person of mighty importance in the house, before he was high enough to look over the table. Wasn't there fireworks on his birthday, and his health drunk with three times three at the tenants' dinner at Christmas! I mind how he used to strut about, toss his head, and bully his nurse, and smash his toys when he got tired of them; and they never pleased him more than a day! He grew older, too old for a nurse, so mistress had a tutor for him. He didn't like a tutor—why should the heir to the estate be plagued with books and study? There was no peace till the tutor was sent off! Master found the boy getting beyond all bounds, with a mighty strong will of his own—sent him to school. He didn't like school—why should the heir be tormented with schooling? He was brought back after the first half, to be a plague to himself and to every one near him! So he grew up, able to settle to nothing, never finishing anything that he began—thinking of nothing but how to kill time! He must go to London and see something of life. So to London he went; and the sharpers crowded around him as the wasps round a ripe plum. They taught him to gamble and spend money—he was apt enough at learning that! The heir to such a fortune was a bird worth the plucking; and such gentry as those that he has brought with him to-day will stick by him while there's one golden feather left! So you see the truth of what I observed," said the butler in conclusion;—"the worst luck which could have befallen young master was to be born the son of a man of fortune. If he'd had his own bread to earn, d'ye see, he'd have studied as a boy, and worked as a man, and thought of something besides pleasure; the sharpers would have left him alone; and he'd have turned out, may be, a mighty respectable member of society."

Mrs. Dale nodded her head very thoughtfully. She was experienced in the management of children, and in her own nursery had always laboured to maintain strict discipline, but she knew well the disadvantages which attend a rich man's son and heir. She sat for a few moments, turning over the matter in her mind, as though the expression of her opinion on the subject could influence the future of the spoilt child of fortune. Then, with the decision of one who has maturely considered a difficult question, and has come to a satisfactory conclusion, she said, "If I were Lady Grange I know what I'd do. I'd send the boy to my own old home. Her brothers are both men of sense and spirit, who would stand no nonsense; and if they didn't bring the young pickle to his senses, why I'm greatly mistaken in the matter."

"Her brothers!" exclaimed cook and lady's-maid in a breath. "Why," said the butler, "don't you know that neither of them ever enters this house?"

Mrs. Dale lifted up her hands in amazement; "Lady Grange quarrelled with her own brothers! impossible!"

"Oh! it's not mistress, but master. The worry and the distress which she has had no words can tell. Why, I don't believe that she may so much as write to her old home!"

"Dear! dear!" exclaimed the old nurse, looking really concerned; "and they were such a happy, united family; it was quite a picture to see them! Miss Clara was the darling of the house; her brothers never thought that they could make enough of their pet. Sure it must be just a heartbreak to her to be on bad terms with them now! How could such a shocking thing have happened?"

"Why, you see," said the butler, laying the finger of his right hand on the palm of his left, and lowering his voice to a more confidential though not less audible tone, "you see it was all along of the marriage settlement. Master thought that mistress should have had more of the money—"

"Throw the money into the sea!" cried Mrs. Dale indignantly; "all the gold in the world is not worth the peace, and union, and love of a family!"

"Oh!" said the butler, "one can't be much in life without seeing how very often money matters break that peace, and union, and love. The purse on one side, the heart on the other, depend on't the purse wins the day."

"There's some truth in that," observed the cook. "My last place was with three old ladies who lived very well and comfortably together, never separated for a day, till some one died and unluckily left them a large fortune to spend. Then they began to find out that their wills could never agree. Miss Jemima liked town, Miss Jessie the country, Miss Martha was all for the sea-side. One must travel this way for health, another that way for amusement;—before six months were over they were all divided, the establishment was broken up; and so I came here."

"Ah!" cried Mrs. Dale sadly, "fortune isn't always sent as a blessing; and where a bad use is made of it, it turns in the end to a curse! There are folk, I daresay, envying my poor lady, thinking that because she has a fine house, fine estate, fine carriage, she must be a happy woman. But well I know that—unless she be much changed from what she was as a child—she would gladly give them all up to see her son a steady, sensible, God-fearing man, and to be happy with her brothers again!"

Jenny having finished her cold meat, now rose and left the house—left it with ideas how changed from those with which she had entered it! The feeling of envy was changed for the feeling of pity; and the young girl, as with light step she made her way towards the home where she was sure of kind smiles and a pleasant welcome, thought how much happier was her own lot than that of the lady of fortune. Even the robe of rich green velvet had lost its attractions for Jenny—was it more beautiful than the fresh turf over which she sped with so light a heart? Her back being now turned to the wind, Jenny no longer felt its keenness; while a brilliant sun was shedding warmth and cheerfulness around. Jenny did not forget to look in the hedges for violets for her little brother. "I daresay," thought she, as she stooped to pluck one from beneath the large green leaves, "I daresay that this sweet little flower will give my Tommy as much pleasure as the rich man's son ever found in his gilded toys. How foolish was I to wish for wealth! Who knows what effect it might have upon me! Mother is right—the best blessings are as free to the poor as to the rich—sunshine for the eyes, love in the home, and a good hope of heaven for the heart! *Better is a dinner of herbs where love is, than a stalled ox and hatred therewith!*"

Ne'er will I sigh for wealth,

Such wealth as coffers can hold:

Contentment, union, and health,

Are not to be bought for gold

The costly treasures I prize

Are treasures of family love—

A happy home here, and the hope so dear

Of a happier home above!

Equally shines the beam

On palace or cottage wall,
The golden rays they stream
To brighten and gladden all!
But, oh! the sunshine I prize
Is the sunshine of family love—
A happy home here, and the hope so dear
Of a happier home above!

The poor no flatterers fear,
They dread no plunderer's art:
When the voice of kindness they hear
They feel it comes from the heart!
Oh! ask the blessing from Heaven,
The blessing of family love—
A happy home here, and the hope so dear
Of a happier home above!

CHAPTER IX.
FALSE FRIENDS.

"Thorns and snares are in the way of the froward."—PROV. xxii. 5.

"Philip, your conduct has distressed me exceedingly," said Lady Grange, laying her hand on the arm of her son, as they entered together the elegant apartment which had been fitted up as her boudoir. "You could not but know my feelings towards those two men, I will not call them gentlemen, whose company you have again forced upon me. You must be aware that your father has shut the doors of this house against them."

"My father has shut the door against better men than they are," said the youth, carelessly; "witness my own uncles Henry and George."

The lip of the lady quivered, the indignant colour rose even to her temples; she attempted to speak, but her voice failed her, and she turned aside to hide her emotion.

"Well, mother, I did not mean to vex you," said Philip, who was rather weak in purpose than hardened in evil; "it *was* a shame to bring Jones and Wildrake here, but—but you see I couldn't help it:" and he played uneasily with his gold-headed riding-whip, while his eye avoided meeting that of his mother.

"They have acquired some strange influence, some mysterious hold over you," answered the lady. "It cannot be," she added anxiously, "that you have broken your promise—that they have drawn you again to the gaming-table—that you are involved in debt to these men?"

Philip whistled an air and sauntered up to the window.

Lady Grange pressed her hand over her eyes, and a sigh, a very heavy sigh, burst from her bosom. Philip heard, and turned impatiently round.

"There's no use in making the worst of matters," said he; "what's done can't be helped, and my debts, such as they are, won't ruin a rich man like my father."

"It is not that which I fear," said the mother faintly, with a terrible consciousness that her son—her hope, her pride, the delight of her heart, had entered on a course which, if persevered in, must end in his ruin both of body and soul. "I tremble at the thought of the misery which you are bringing on yourself. These men are making you their victim: they are blinding your eyes; they are throwing a net around you, and you have not the resolution to break from the snare."

"They are very pleasant, jovial fellows!" cried Philip, trying to hide under an appearance of careless gaiety the real annoyance which he felt at the words of his mother. "I've asked them to dine here to-day, and—"

"*I* shall not appear at the table," said Lady Grange, drawing herself up with dignity; "and if your father should arrive—"

"Oh! he won't arrive to-night; he never travels so late."

"But Philip," said the lady earnestly, again laying her cold hand on his arm—she was interrupted by her wayward and undutiful son.

"Mother, there's no use in saying anything more on the subject; it only worries you, and puts me out of temper. I can't, and I won't, be uncivil to my friends;" and turning hastily round, Philip quitted the apartment.

"Friends!" faintly echoed Lady Grange, as she saw the door close behind her misguided son. "Oh!" she exclaimed, throwing herself on a sofa, and burying her face, "was there ever a mother—ever a woman so unhappy as I am!"

Her cup was indeed very bitter; it was one which the luxuries which surrounded her had not the least power to sweeten. Her husband was a man possessing many noble qualities both of head and heart; but the fatal love of gold, like those petrifying springs which change living twigs to dead stone, had made him hardened, quarrelsome, and worldly. It had drawn him away from the worship of his God; for there is deep truth in the declaration of the apostle, that the covetous man is *an idolater*. It was this miserable love of gold which had induced Sir Gilbert to break with the family of his wife, and separate her from those to whom her loving heart still clung with the fondest affection. Lady Grange yearned for a sight of her early home; but gold had raised a barrier between her and the companions of her childhood. And what had the possession of gold done for the man who made it his idol? It had put snares in the path of his only son; it had made the weakminded but headstrong youth be entrapped by the wicked for the sake of his wealth, as the ermine is hunted down for its rich fur. It had given to himself heavy responsibilities, for which he would have to answer at the bar of Heaven; for from him unto whom much has been given, much at the last day will be required.

Yes, Lady Grange was very miserable. And how did she endeavour to lighten the burden of her misery? Was it by counting over her jewels—looking at the costly and beautiful things which adorned her dwelling—thinking of her carriages and horses and glittering plate, or the number of her rich and titled friends? No; she sought comfort where widow Green had sought it, when her child lay dangerously ill, and there was neither a loaf on her shelf nor a penny in her purse. The rich lady did what the poor one had done—she fell on her knees and with tears poured out her heart to the merciful Father of all. She told Him her sorrows, she told Him her fears; she asked Him for that help which she so much required. Her case was a harder one than the widow's. A visit from the clergyman, a present from a benevolent friend, God's blessing on a simple remedy, had soon changed Mrs. Green's sorrow into joy. The anguish of Lady Grange lay deeper; her faith was more sorely tried; her fears were not for the bodies, but the souls of those whom she loved;—and where is the mortal who can give us a cure for the disease of sin?

While his mother was weeping and praying, Philip was revelling and drinking. Fast were the bottles pushed round, and often were the glasses refilled. The stately banqueting-room resounded with laughter and merriment; and as the evening advanced, with boisterous song. It was late before the young men quitted the table, and then, heated with wine, they threw the window wide open, to let the freshness of the night air cool their fevered temples.

Beautiful looked the park in the calm moonlight. Not a breath stirred the branches of the trees, their dark shadows lay motionless on the green-sward: perfect silence and stillness reigned around. But the holy quietness of nature was rudely disturbed by the voices of the revellers.

With the conversation that passed I shall not soil my pages. The window opened into a broad stone balcony, and seating themselves upon its parapet, the young men exchanged stories and jests. After many sallies of so-called wit, Wildrake rallied Philip on the quantity of wine which he had taken, and betted that he could not walk steadily from the one end of the balcony to the other. Philip, with that insane pride which can plume itself on being *mighty to mingle strong drink*, maintained that his head was as clear, and his faculties as perfect, as though he had tasted nothing but water; and declared that he could walk round the edge of the parapet with as steady a step as he would tread the gravel-path in the morning!

Wildrake laughed, and dared him to do it; Jones betted ten to one that he could not.

"Done!" cried Philip, and sprang up on the parapet in a moment!

"Come down again!" called out Wildrake, who had enough of sense left to perceive the folly and danger of the wager.

Philip did not appear to hear him. Attempting to balance himself by his arms, with a slow and unsteady step he began to make his way along the lofty and narrow edge.

The two young men held their breath. To one who with unsteady feet walks the slippery margin of temptation the higher his position, the greater his danger; the loftier his elevation, the more perilous a fall!

"He will never get to the end!" said Jones, watching with some anxiety the movements of his companion.

The words had scarcely escaped his lips when they received a startling fulfilment. Philip had not proceeded half way along the parapet when a slight sound in the garden below him attracted his attention. He glanced down for a moment: and there, in the cold, clear moonlight, gazing sternly upon him, he beheld his father! The sudden start of surprise which he gave threw the youth off his balance—he staggered back, lost his footing, stretched out his hands wildly to save himself, and fell with a loud cry to the ground!

All was now confusion and terror. There were the rushing of footsteps hither and thither, voices calling, bells loudly ringing—and, above all, the voice of a mother's anguish, piercing to the soul! Jones and Wildrake hurried off to the stables, saddled their horses themselves, and dashed off at full speed to summon a surgeon, glad of any excuse to make their escape from the place.

The unfortunate Philip was raised from the ground, and carried into the house. His groans showed the severity of his sufferings. The slightest motion was to him torture, and an hour of intense suspense ensued, before the arrival of the surgeon. Lady Grange made a painful effort to be calm. She thought of everything, did all that she could do for the relief of her son, and even strove to speak words of comfort and hope to her husband, who appeared almost stupified by his sorrow. Prayer was still her support—prayer, silent, but almost unceasing.

The surgeon arrived—the injuries received by the sufferer were examined, though it was long before Philip, unaccustomed to pain and incapable of self-control, would permit necessary measures to be taken. His resistance greatly added to his sufferings. He had sustained a compound fracture of his leg, besides numerous bruises and contusions. The broken bone had to be set, and the pale mother stood by, longing, in the fervour of her unselfish love, that she could endure the agony in the place of her son. The pampered child of luxury shrank sensitively from pain, and the thought that he had brought all his misery upon himself by his folly and disobedience rendered it yet more intolerable. When the surgeon had at length done his work, Lady Grange retired with him to another apartment, and, struggling to command her choking voice, asked him the question on the reply to which all her earthly happiness seemed to hang—whether he had hope that the life of her boy might be spared.

"I have every hope," said the surgeon, cheerfully, "if we can keep down the fever." Then, for the first time since she had seen her son lie bleeding before her, the mother found the relief of tears.

Through the long night she quitted not the sufferer's pillow, bathing his fevered brow, relieving his thirst, whispering comfort to his troubled spirit. Soon after daybreak Philip sank into a quiet, refreshing sleep; and Lady Grange, feeling as if a mountain's weight had been lifted from her heart, hurried to carry the good news to her husband.

She found him in the spacious saloon, pacing restlessly to and fro. His brow was knit, his lips compressed; his disordered dress and haggard countenance showed that he, too, had watched the live-long night.

"He sleeps at last, Gilbert, thank God!" Her face brightened as she spoke; but there was no corresponding look of joy on that of her husband.

"Gilbert, the doctor assures me that there is every prospect of our dear boy's restoration!"

"And to what is he to be restored?" said the father gloomily; "to poverty—misery—ruin?"

Lady Grange stood mute with surprise, scarcely believing the evidence of her senses, almost deeming that the words must have been uttered in a dream. But it was no dream, but one of those strange, stern realities which we meet with in life. Her husband indeed stood before her a ruined man! A commercial crash, like those which have so often reduced the rich to poverty, coming almost as suddenly as the earthquake which shakes the natural world, had overthrown all his fortune! The riches in which he had trusted had taken to themselves wings and flown away!

Here was another startling shock; but Lady Grange felt it far less than the first. It seemed to her that if her son were only spared to her, she could bear cheerfully any other trial. When riches had increased she had not set her heart upon them; she had endeavoured to spend them as a good steward of God, and to lay up treasure in that blessed place where there is no danger of its ever being lost. Sir Gilbert was far more crushed than his wife was by this misfortune. He saw his idol broken before his eyes, and where was he to turn for comfort? Everything upon which his eye rested was a source of pain to him; for must he not part with all, leave all in which his heart had delighted, all in which his soul had taken pride? He forgot that poverty was only forestalling by a few years the inevitable work of death!

The day passed wearily away. Philip suffered much pain, was weak and low, and bitterly conscious how well he had earned the misery which he was called on to endure. It was a mercy that he was experiencing, before it was too late, *that thorns and snares are in the way of the froward.* He liked his mother to read the Bible to him, just a few verses at a time, as he had strength to bear it; and in this occupation she herself found the comfort which she needed. Sir Gilbert, full of his own troubles, scarcely ever entered the apartment of his son.

Towards evening a servant came softly into the sickroom, bringing a sealed letter for her lady. There was no post-mark upon it, and the girl informed her mistress that the gentleman who had brought it was waiting in the garden for a reply. The first glance at the hand-writing, at the well-known seal, brought colour to the cheek of the lady. But it was a hand-writing which she had been forbidden to read! it was a seal which she must not break! She motioned to the maid to take her place beside the invalid, who happened at that moment to be sleeping, and with a quick step and a throbbing heart she hurried away to find her husband.

He was in his study, his arms resting on his open desk, and his head bowed down upon them. Bills and papers, scattered in profusion on the table, showed what had been the nature of the occupation which he had not had the courage to finish. He started from his posture of despair as his wife laid a gentle touch on his shoulder, and, without uttering a word, she placed the unopened letter in his hand.

My reader shall have the privilege of looking over Sir Gilbert's shoulder, and perusing the contents of that letter:—

"DEAREST SISTER,—We have heard of your trials, and warmly sympathize in your sorrow. Let Sir Gilbert know that we have placed at his banker's, after having settled it upon you, double the sum which caused our unhappy differences. Let the past be forgotten; let us again meet as those should meet who have gathered together round the same hearth, mourned over the same grave, and shared joys and sorrows together, as it is our anxious desire to do now. I shall be my own messenger, and shall wait in person to receive your reply.—Your ever attached brother,

HENRY LATOUR."

A few minutes more and Lady Grange was in the arms of her brother; while Sir Gilbert was silently grasping the hand of one whom, but for misfortune, he would never have known as a friend.

All the neighbourhood pitied the gentle lady, the benefactress of the poor, when she dismissed her servants, sold her jewels, and quitted her beautiful home to seek a humbler shelter. Amongst the hundreds who crowded to the public auction of the magnificent furniture and plate, which had been the admiration of all who had seen them, many thought with compassion of the late owners, reduced to such sudden poverty, though the generosity of the lady's family had saved them from want or dependence.

And yet truly, never since her marriage had Lady Grange been less an object of compassion.

Her son was slowly but surely recovering, and his preservation from meeting sudden death unprepared, was to her a source of unutterable thankfulness. Her own family appeared to regard her with even more tender affection than if no coldness had ever arisen between them; and their love was to her beyond price. Even Sir Gilbert's harsh, worldly character was somewhat softened by trials, and by the unmerited kindness which he met with from those whom, in his prosperity, he had slighted and shunned. Lady Grange felt that her prayers had been answered indeed, though in a way very different from what she had hoped or expected. The chain by which her son had been gradually drawn down towards ruin, by those who sought his company for the sake of his money, had been suddenly snapped by the loss of his fortune. The weak youth was left to the guidance of those to whom his welfare was really dear. Philip, obliged to rouse himself from his indolence, and exert himself to earn his living, became a far wiser and more estimable man than he would ever have been as the heir to a fortune; and he never forgot the lesson which pain, weakness, and shame had taught him—that the way of evil is also the way of sorrow: *Thorns and snares are in the way of the froward.*

Who Wisdom's path forsakes,

Leaves all true joy behind:

He who the peace of others breaks,

No peace himself shall find.

Flowers above and thorns below,

Little pleasure, lasting woe—

Such is the fate that sinners know!

The drunkard gaily sings

Above his foaming glass

But shame and pain the revel brings,

Ere many hours can pass.

Flowers above and thorns below,

Little pleasure, lasting woe—

Such is the fate that sinners know!

The thief may count his gains;—
If he the sum could see
Of future punishment and pains,
Sad would his reckoning be!
Flowers above and thorns below,
Little pleasure, lasting woe—
Such is the fate that sinners know!

The Sabbath-breaker spurns
What Wisdom did ordain:
God's rest to Satan's use he turns—
A blessing to a bane.
Flowers above and thorns below,
Little pleasure, lasting woe—
Such is the fate that sinners know!

O Lord, to Thee we pray;
Do Thou our faith increase!
Help us to walk in Wisdom's way—
The only way of peace!
For flowers above and thorns below,
Little pleasure, lasting woe—
Such is the fate that sinners know!

CHAPTER X.
COURAGE AND CANDOUR.

"The fear of man bringeth a snare; but whoso putteth his trust in the Lord shall be safe."—PROV. xxix. 25.

Jonas Colter was as gallant an old seaman as ever sailed on salt water. He was kind and generous, also, and would have shared his last shilling or his last crust with any poor creature who required it. Jonas loved his Bible and loved his church, and might have been seen regularly every Sunday morning with his book under his arm stumping along with his wooden leg, on his way to the house of prayer. But Jonas had one sad failing—rather should I call it one great sin, for *an angry man stirreth up strife, and a furious man aboundeth in transgression.* He had no sort of command over his temper, and that temper was an uncommonly bad one.

"There are many excuses to be made for him," his sister, Mrs. Morris, would often say. "Just think what a rough life he has led, and how much he has had to suffer. If his temper rises sometimes like a gale of wind, like a gale of wind it is soon over!"

"But, like a gale of wind, it leaves its effects behind it!" observed a neighbour, when this remark was repeated to him. "I shan't care to call often at Mrs. Morris's house while her bear of a brother makes it his den!"

There were perhaps none on earth whom Jonas loved better than Johnny and Alie, the children of his sister; and yet none suffered more from his fierce and ungoverned temper. They feared him more than they loved him; and notwithstanding the many little presents which he made them, and the many little kindnesses which he showed them, his absence, when he left home, was always felt as a relief. It is impossible to regard with the greatest affection one who puts you in perpetual fear, or to feel quite happy with a companion whose smile may in a moment be changed to a frown, whose pleasant talk to a passionate burst.

Johnny, though considered a courageous boy, was afraid of rousing his uncle; and if to him Jonas was an object of fear, to Alie he was an object of terror. Alie was one of the most timid little creatures in the village. She would go a long way round to avoid passing a large dog, was uneasy at the sight of a turkey-cock, and never dared so much as raise her eyes if a stranger happened to address her. It was not only from the temper of her uncle that poor little Alie now suffered; Johnny, while himself annoyed at the roughness of Jonas, with the imitative disposition of youth, began in a certain degree to copy it. He knew that the old sailor was thought generous and brave, and therefore wished to be like him; but made the very common mistake of imitators—followed him rather in his defects than in those things which were worthy of admiration. Perhaps Johnny also tried to hide from himself and others how much he was cowed by his uncle, by assuming a blustering manner himself. This is so often unconsciously done, that whenever I see a bully I am inclined to suspect that I am looking at a coward.

Alie was fond of listening to her uncle's sea-stories—"long yarns," as he called them—but only if she could listen unobserved. Her favourite place was the window-seat, where she could draw the curtain before her to screen her from observation. To be suddenly addressed by her uncle was enough to make the timid child start.

Jonas had many curiosities from foreign parts, which it amused the children to see—dried sea-weed, reptiles in bottles, odd specimens of work done in straw by savages in some distant islands with unpronounceable names. These treasures were never kept under lock and key; it was quite enough that they belonged to the terrible Jonas; no one was likely to meddle much with his goods, lest he should "give 'em a bit of his mind."

"Alie," cried Johnny one morning, when the children happened to be alone in their uncle's little room, "where on earth have you put my 'Robinson Crusoe?'"

"I?" said the little girl, looking up innocently from her work; "I have not so much as seen it."

"Look for it, then!" cried the boy, in the loud coarse tone which he had too faithfully copied from his uncle.

Little Alie was plying her needle diligently, and her brother had nothing to do; but she was much too timid to remonstrate. She set down her work, and moved quietly about the room, glancing behind this thing and under that; while Johnny, stretched at full length on the floor, amused himself with chucking up marbles.

"There it is!" cried Alie at last, glancing upwards at a high shelf, on which were ranged divers of Jonas's bottles.

"Get it down!" said the boy, who, to judge by his tone, thought himself equal to an admiral, at the least.

"I don't think that I can," replied Alie; "I can't reach the shelf, and there's another book and a heavy bottle too on the top of 'Robinson Crusoe.'"

"Goose! can't you get a chair?" was the only reply vouchsafed.

Alie slowly dragged a heavy chair to the spot, while Johnny commenced singing—

"Britons never, never shall be slaves!"

considering of course as exceptions to the rule all gentle, helpless, little British girls, who happen to have strong, tyrannical brothers.

"There!—mind!—take care what you're about!" he cried, as he watched Alie's efforts to accomplish the task for which she had hardly sufficient strength or height. Scarcely were the words uttered when down with a crash came the bottle and the books, almost upsetting poor Alie herself!

Johnny jumped up from the ground in an instant.

"What is to be done!" he exclaimed, looking with dismay at the broken bottle, whose green contents, escaping in all directions, was staining the floor and also the book, which was one of Jonas's greatest treasures.

"Oh! what is to be done!" repeated poor Alie, in real distress.

Johnny felt so angry with himself, that he was much inclined, after his usual fashion, to vent his anger upon his sister. Seeing, however, that they were both in the same trouble, and that it had been occasioned by his laziness in making the little girl do what he ought to have done himself, he repressed his indignation, and turned his mind to the means of remedying the evil.

"My uncle will be in a downright tempest!" he exclaimed; "what say you to a good long walk right off to the farm, to get out of the way of its fury?"

"It would be just as bad when we came back!" said Alie dolefully, stooping to pick up the injured book.

"Don't touch it!" cried Johnny authoritatively; "don't get the stain on your dress as well as on everything else. I have hit on a famous plan. We'll shut up the cat in the room, then go on our walk, and no one on earth will guess that she did not do the mischief."

"Oh! but, Johnny, would it be right?"

"Right! fiddlestick!" cried the boy. "Put on your bonnet and be quick, while I look for Tabby in the kitchen."

Alie had great doubts whether she ought to obey, but she was frightened and confused, and accustomed to submit to the orders of her brother; and, after all, her uncle was so fond of the cat, that it was likely to suffer much less from his anger than any other creature would have done.

Tabby was soon caught, and placed on the floor near the broken bottle. Johnny dipped one of her paws in the fluid, to serve as further evidence against her, and then came out of the little room.

"I must get out my work—I left it there," said Alie.

"Go in quickly, and get it then," replied Johnny.

ALIE WATCHING THE CAT.

Alie went in, and returned with the work, but stood hesitating before she quitted the room, looking back with her hand on the lock.

"Oh, Johnny! Tabby is licking it up!"

"So much the better!" cried he; "her whiskers will tell tales of her then!"

"But, Johnny—"

"Come quickly! I can't stand waiting for you all the day!" exclaimed the boy; "uncle may be back before we get off!"

These words quickened the movements of Alie: she closed the door with a sigh.

Very grave and silent was the child during the whole of that long walk; very grave and silent during her visit to the farm. Johnny first laughed at her nonsense, as he called it, and then grew irritable and rude, after the example of his uncle. The walk home was a very unpleasant one to Alie.

"POOR TABBY!"

But more unpleasant was the arrival at home. The first sight which met the children's eyes, on their return, was poor Tabby stretched out lifeless on the floor of the kitchen, and their uncle bending over her with a flushed face and knitted brow; while their mother, who stood beside him, was vainly endeavouring to calm him.

"Accidents will occur, dear brother—"

"There has been gross carelessness somewhere," growled the sailor; and turning suddenly round toward the children, whom he now first perceived, he thundered out to Johnny, "Was it you, sir, who shut the cat into my room?"

"No," answered Johnny very promptly: then he added, "Alie and I have been out a long time; we have been all the way to the farm."

"I may have shut the door myself," said the mother, "without knowing of the cat being in the place." And, to turn the sailor's mind from his loss, she continued, "I'm going up to the village, Jonas, and I've a very large basket to carry; Johnny's just come off a long walk, or—"

"I'm your man!" cried the sailor; "I'll help you with your load. Just wait a few minutes till I've buried this poor thing in the garden. I shouldn't like the dogs to get at her—though she's past feeling now, poor Tabby!" And as the stern, rough man stooped, raised his dead favourite, and carried it away, Alie thought that she saw something like moisture trembling in his eye.

"Alie," said her mother, "go into that room, and carefully collect the broken pieces of the bottle which poor Tabby managed to knock off the shelf; and wash that part of the floor which is stained by the liquid: be attentive not to leave a drop of it anywhere; for the contents of the bottle was deadly poison, and I cannot be too thankful that the cat was the only sufferer."

Alie obeyed with a very heavy heart. She was grieved at the death of Tabby, grieved at the vexation of her uncle—most grieved of all at the thought that she had not acted openly and conscientiously herself.

When she returned to the kitchen, she found Johnny its only occupant, her mother and uncle having set off for the village.

"I say, Alie," cried Johnny, "wasn't it lucky that uncle asked me instead of you about shutting the cat in? 'Twas you that closed the door, you know."

"Oh, Johnny!" said his sister, "I feel so unhappy about it! I wish that I had told mother everything—I don't think that I could have spoken to uncle. It seems just as if I were deceiving them both!"

"Nonsense!" cried Johnny, in a very loud tone; "you ought to be too happy that the storm has blown over!"

But the conscience of Alie would make itself heard, notwithstanding her brother's voice of scorn. She had been accustomed from the time when she could first talk, to speak the simple truth, and the whole truth. She knew that there may be falsehood even in *silence*, when that silence tends to deceive. She felt that she had wronged her uncle, by destroying his property, and, however unintentionally, causing the death of his pet; and instead of frankly confessing the wrong, and asking pardon, she was concealing the matter. Alie went slowly up to her own little room, took down from its shelf her well-used Bible—that would be a safer counsellor than her brother! She opened it, and the first verse upon which her eyes rested was this, *The fear of man bringeth a snare: but whoso putteth his trust in the Lord shall be safe.* Alie closed her book, and resting her head upon her hand, sat and thought:—

"Mother has often told me that the language of heaven is truth, and that whosoever *loveth or maketh a lie* shall never be admitted to that happy place! But why should my mind be so troubled?—I have not said a single word that is not true. But I have concealed the truth. And why?—because of *the fear of man*, which the Bible tells me *bringeth a snare.* What then would be my straight course of duty? to confess that I threw down the poison? Would not that bring my brother into trouble? No; for it was I who climbed on the chair, I who knocked over the bottle, I who last shut the door—all the mischief was done by me, though it was not done for my own pleasure. I know what will be my best plan," said Alie, with a sigh of relief at coming to anything like a decision: "I'll confess all to mother when she comes back from the village; and she will choose a good time, when my uncle is in a pleasant temper and I am out of the way, and tell him that I killed poor Tabby, but am exceedingly sorry that I did it."

So Alie returned to the kitchen, and put on the water to boil for tea and sat down to her unfinished work, awaiting her mother's return. Her heart beat faster than usual when she heard the clump, clump of her uncle's wooden leg, but still more when he entered the house alone.

"Where's mother?" said Johnny.

"She's gone to the vicarage," replied Jonas. "She met a messenger to tell her that the lady there is taken very ill, and wants some one to nurse her; so she sheered off straight for Brampton, and desired me to come back and tell you."

"When will she return?" asked Alie with anxiety.

"That's when the lady gets better, I s'pose. I suspect that she's cast anchor for a good while, from what I hear," replied the sailor. "But pluck up a good heart, little lass, and don't look as though you were about to set the water-works going; I've brought you something to cheer you up a bit;" and slowly unfolding his red pocket-handkerchief, Jonas displayed a large cake of gingerbread. "Here's for you," he said, holding it out to his niece.

"Oh! uncle!" cried Alie, without attempting to touch it.

"Take it, will you," said he sharply; "what are ye hanging back for?" Alie took the cake, and thanked her uncle in a faltering voice. Jonas stooped down, lighted his pipe, and as he glanced at the warm corner which used to be his favourite's chosen place, and missed her well-known purr, the old sailor gave an unconscious sigh, and "Poor Tabby!" escaped from his lips.

UNCLE JONAS.

The sound of the sigh, and the words, gave pain to the heart of little Alie. "Here am I receiving kindness from my uncle," thought she, "and knowing how little I deserve it; and yet I have not courage to confess the truth! I am sure that fear is *a snare* to me. Oh, that I had a braver heart, so that I should dread nothing but doing wrong! Johnny is as bold as a lion, yet I am sure that even he would be afraid to tell the truth to my uncle!"

"What's the matter with the lass?" cried Jonas with blunt kindness, taking the pipe from his lips, and looking steadily at the child. "Ye're vexed at your mother biding away?"

"It is not that," replied Alie, very softly.

"Ye're fretting about the cat?"

"Partly," murmured the child.

"Kind little soul!" exclaimed the sailor, heartily: "I'll get a white kitten, or a tortoise-shell for ye, if one's to be had for love or money! But maybe ye're like the Jack-tar, and don't think new friends like the old!" and the rough hard hand of the seaman was laid caressingly on the little girl's shoulder.

"Uncle, you quite mistake me, you—you—would not be so kind if you knew all!" said Alie rapidly. The first difficult step was taken, but poor Alie's cheek was crimson, and she would have felt it at that moment impossible to have raised her eyes from the floor.

"What's all this?" exclaimed Jonas roughly, while Johnny, afraid that the whole truth was coming out, made a hasty retreat from the kitchen.

"What's all this?" repeated the bluff sailor. Alie had now gone so far that she had not power to retreat. Her little hands pressed tightly together, her voice tremulous and indistinct with fear, she stammered forth, "It was I who knocked down the bottle—and—and shut poor Tabby into your room—and—"

"Shut her in on purpose?" thundered Jonas, starting up from his seat. Alie bent her head as her only reply.

"Shut in the cat that the blame might be laid upon her!—took a long walk that the mean trick might be successful!" At each sentence his voice rose louder and louder, so that Johnny could hear it at the other side of the road, while poor Alie bent like a reed beneath the storm.

"And was your brother with you, girl?" continued the angry sailor, after a short but terrible pause.

Poor Alie was dreadfully perplexed; she squeezed her hands together tighter than ever; she could not speak, but her silence spoke enough.

"Mean coward!" exclaimed Jonas, striking the table with his clenched fist till it rang again; "and he has set all sail, and made off, and left this little pinnace to brave the storm alone!" Alie burst into tears; and whether it was the sight of these tears, or whether his own words reminded the sailor that Alie at least had now acted an honest, straight-forward part, his anger towards her was gone in a moment, and he drew her kindly to his knee.

"Dry these eyes, and think no more about it," said he; "you never guessed that the liquid was poison, and accidents, as they say, will happen even in the best-regulated families. But why did not you and your sneak of a brother tell me honestly about breaking the bottle, instead of playing such a cowardly trick as that of shutting up the poor cat in the room?"

"Oh, uncle," murmured Alie, at length finding her voice, "we knew that you would be so dreadfully angry!"

"Humph!" said the sailor thoughtfully. "So the fear of me was a snare to you. Well, you may go after your brother, if he's not run away so far that you cannot find him, and tell him that he may sneak back as soon as he can muster enough of courage, for not a word, good or bad, shall he hear from me about the bottle or the cat. And mind you, my honest little lass," continued Jonas, "I'll not forget the white kitten for you;—for though you've not a stout heart you've a brave conscience, and dare speak the truth even to a crabbed old sailor, who you knew would be 'so dreadfully angry.'"

Alie flew off like a bird, her heart lightened of its load, and rejoicing in the consciousness that a painful duty had been performed. And whenever in future life she felt tempted to take a crooked course from the dread of some peril in the straight one, the timid girl found courage in remembering the verse which had struck her so much on that day—*The fear of man bringeth a snare: but whoso putteth his trust in the Lord shall be safe.*

The fear of God most high—

It is a holy fear;

It makes us pass through life as those

Who know their Judge is near.

The fear of sinful Man—

'Tis a debasing fear;

Shame will be theirs who dare not brave

A censure or a sneer!

It was the fear of God

Through which the Hebrews three

Undaunted met the tyrant's frown,

Unmoved the flames could see!

It was the fear of Man

Weak Pilate's breast within,

That stained his hands with guiltless blood,

His soul with blackest sin!

No courage is like that

Which steadfast faith bestows;

With God our friend, we would be safe

Were all the world our foes!

Faith but the duty sees,

Where doubt would danger scan:

'Tis through the fear of God alone

We crush the fear of Man!

CHAPTER XI.
THE SAILOR'S RESOLVE.

"An angry man stirreth up strife, and a furious man aboundeth in transgression."—PROV. xxix. 22.

The old sailor Jonas sat before the fire with his pipe in his mouth, looking steadfastly into the glowing coals. Not that, following a favourite practice of his little niece, he was making out red-hot castles and flaming buildings in the grate, or that his thoughts were in any way connected with the embers: he was doing what it would be well if we all sometimes did—looking into himself, and reflecting on what had happened in relation to his own conduct.

"So," thought he, "here am I, an honest old fellow—I may say it, with all my faults; and one who shrinks from falsehood more than from fire; and I find that I, with my bearish temper, am actually driving those about me into it—teaching them to be crafty, tricky, and cowardly! I knew well enough that my gruffness plagued others, but I never saw how it *tempted* others until now; tempted them to meanness, I would say, for I have found a thousand times that *an angry man stirreth up strife*, and that a short word may begin a long quarrel. I am afraid that I have not thought enough on this matter. I've looked on bad temper as a very little sin, and I begin to suspect that it is a great one, both in God's eyes and in the consequences that it brings. Let me see if I can reckon up its evils! It makes those miserable whom one would wish to make happy; it often, like an adverse gale, forces them to back instead of steering straight for the port. It dishonours one's profession, lowers one's flag, makes the world mock at the religion which can leave a man as rough and rugged as a heathen savage. It's directly contrary to the Word of God—it's wide as east from west of the example set before us! Yes, a furious temper is a very evil thing; I'd give my other leg to be rid of mine!" and in the warmth of his self-reproach the sailor struck his wooden one against the hearth with such violence as to make Alie start in terror that some fierce explosion was about to follow.

"Well, I've made up my mind as to its being an evil—a great evil," continued Jonas, in his quiet meditation; "the next question is, how is the evil to be got rid of? There's the pinch! It clings to one like one's skin. It's one's nature—how can one fight against nature? And yet, I take it, it's the very business of faith to conquer our evil nature. As I read somewhere, any dead dog can float with the stream, it's the living dog that swims against it. I mind the trouble I had about the wicked habit of swearing, when first I took to trying to serve God and leave off my evil courses. Bad words came to my mouth as natural as the very air that I breathed. What did I do to cure myself of that evil? Why, I resolved again and again, and found that my resolutions were always snapping like a rotten cable in a storm; and I was driven from my anchorage so often, that I almost began to despair. Then I prayed hard to be helped; and I said to myself, 'God helps those who help themselves, and maybe if I determine to do something that I should be sorry to do, every time that an oath comes from my mouth, it would assist me to remember my duty.' I resolved to break my pipe the first time that I swore; and I've never uttered an oath from that day to this, not even in my most towering passions! Now I'll try the same cure again; not to punish a sin, but to prevent it. If I fly into a fury, I'll break my pipe! There, Jonas Grimstone, I give you fair warning!" and the old sailor smiled grimly to himself, and stirred the fire with an air of satisfaction.

Not one rough word did Jonas utter that evening—indeed he was remarkably silent; for the simplest way of saying nothing evil, he thought, was to say nothing at all. Jonas looked with much pleasure at his pipe, when he put it on the mantelpiece for the night. "You've weathered this day, old friend," said he; "we'll be on the look-out against squalls to-morrow."

The next morning Jonas occupied himself in his own room with his phials, and his nephew and niece were engaged in the kitchen in preparing for the Sunday school, which their mother made them regularly attend. The door was open between the two rooms, and, as the place was not large, Jonas heard every word that passed between Johnny and Alie almost as well as if he had been close beside them.

Johnny. I say, Alie—

Alie. Please, Johnny, let me learn this quietly. If I do not know it my teacher will be vexed. My work being behind-hand yesterday has put me quite back with my tasks. You know that I cannot learn as fast as you do.

Johnny. Oh! you've plenty of time. I want you to do something for me. Do you know that I have lost my new ball?

Alie. Why, I saw you take it out of your pocket yesterday, just after we crossed the stile on our way back from the farm.

Johnny. That's it! I took it out of my pocket, and I never put it in again. I want you to go directly and look for the ball. That stile is only three fields off, you know. You must look carefully along the path all the way; and lose no time, or some one else may pick it up.

Alie. Pray, Johnny, don't ask me to go into the fields.

Johnny. I tell you, you have plenty of time for your lessons.

Alie. It is not that, but—

Johnny. Speak out, will you?

Alie. You know—there are—cows!

Johnny burst into a loud, coarse laugh of derision. "You miserable little coward!" he cried, "I'd like to see one chasing you round the meadow! How you'd scamper! how you'd scream! rare fun it would be—ha, ha, ha!"

"Rare fun would it be, sir!" exclaimed an indignant voice, as Jonas stumped from the next room, and, seizing his nephew by the collar of his jacket, gave him a hearty shake; "rare fun would it be—and what do you call this? You dare twit your sister with cowardice!—you who sneaked off yesterday like a fox because you had not the spirit to look an old man in the face!—you who bully the weak and cringe to the strong!—you who have the manners of a bear with the heart of a pigeon!" Every sentence was accompanied by a violent shake, which almost took the breath from the boy; and Jonas, red with passion, concluded his speech by flinging Johnny from him with such force that, but for the wall against which he staggered, he must have fallen to the ground.

The next minute Jonas walked up to the mantelpiece, and exclaiming, in a tone of vexation, "Run aground again!" took his pipe, snapped it in two, and flung the pieces into the fire. He then stumped back to his room, slamming the door behind him.

"The old fury!" muttered the panting Johnny between his clenched teeth, looking fiercely towards his uncle's room.

"To break his own pipe!" exclaimed Alie. "I never knew him do anything like that before, however angry he might be!"

Johnny took down his cap from its peg, and, in as ill humour as can well be imagined, went out to search for his ball. He took what revenge he could on his formidable uncle, while amusing himself that afternoon by looking over his "Robinson Crusoe." Johnny was fond of his pencil, though he had never learned to draw; and the margins of his books were often adorned with grim heads or odd figures, by his hand. There was a picture in "Robinson Crusoe" representing a party of cannibals, as hideous as fancy could represent them, dancing around their fire. Johnny diverted his mind, and gratified his malice, by doing his best so to alter the foremost figure as to make him appear with a wooden leg, while he drew on his head a straw hat, unmistakably like that of the old sailor, and touched up the features so as to give a dim resemblance to his face. To prevent a doubt as to the meaning of the sketch, Johnny scribbled on the side of the picture,—

"In search of fierce savages no one need roam;

The fiercest and ugliest, you'll find him at home!"

He secretly showed the picture to Alie.

"Oh, Johnny, how naughty! What would uncle say if he saw it?"

"We might look out for squalls indeed! but uncle never by any chance looks at a book of that sort."

"I think that you had better rub out the pencilling as fast as you can," said Alie.

"Catch me rubbing it out!" cried Johnny; "it's the best sketch that ever I drew, and as like the old savage as it can stare!"

Late in the evening Mrs. Morris returned, a nurse from London having been sent for the lady. Right glad were Johnny and Alie to see her sooner than they had ventured to expect. She brought them a few oranges, to show her remembrance of them. Nor was the old sailor forgotten; carefully she drew from her bag, and presented to him, a new pipe.

The children glanced at each other. Jonas took the pipe with a curious expression on his face, which his sister was at a loss to understand.

"Thank'ee kindly," he said; "I see it'll be a case of—

"'If ye try and don't succeed,

Try, try, try, again,'"

What he meant was a riddle to every one else present, although not to the reader.

The "try" was very successful on that evening and the following day. Never had Johnny and Alie found their uncle so agreeable. His manner almost approached to gentleness—it was a calm after a storm.

"Uncle is so very good and kind," said Alie to her brother, as they walked home from afternoon service, "that I wonder how you can bear to have that naughty picture still in your book. He is not in the least like a cannibal, and it seems quite wrong to laugh at him so."

"I'll rub it all out one of these days," replied Johnny; "but I must show it first to Peter Crane. He says that I never hit on a likeness: if he sees that, he'll never say so again!"

The next morning Jonas occupied himself with gathering wild-flowers and herbs in the fields. He carried them into his little room, where Johnny heard him whistling "Old Tom Bowling," like one at peace with himself and all the world.

Presently Jonas called to the boy to bring him a knife from the kitchen; a request made in an unusually courteous tone of voice, and with which, of course, Johnny immediately complied.

He found Jonas busy drying his plants, by laying them neatly between the pages of a book, preparatory to pressing them down. What was the terror of Johnny when he perceived that the book whose pages Jonas was turning over for this purpose was no other than his "Robinson Crusoe!"

"Oh, if I could only get it out of his hands before he comes to that horrid picture! Oh, what shall I do! what shall I do!" thought the bewildered Johnny. "Uncle, I was reading that book," at last he mustered courage to say aloud.

"You may read it again to-morrow," was the quiet reply of Jonas.

"Perhaps he will not look at that picture," reflected Johnny. "I wish that I could see exactly which part of the book he is at! He looks too quiet a great deal for any mischief to have been done yet! Dear! dear! I would give anything to have that 'Robinson Crusoe' at the bottom of the sea! I do think that my uncle's face is growing very red!—yes; the veins on his forehead are swelling! Depend on't he's turned over to those unlucky cannibals, and will be ready to eat me like one of them! I'd better make off before the thunder-clap comes!"

"Going to sheer off again, Master Johnny?" said the old sailor, in a very peculiar tone of voice, looking up from the open book on which his finger now rested.

"I've a little business," stammered out Johnny.

"Yes, a little business with me, which you'd better square before you hoist sail. Why, when you made such a good figure of this savage, did you not clap jacket and boots on this little cannibal beside him, and make a pair of 'em 'at home'? I suspect you and I are both in the same boat as far as regards our tempers, my lad!"

Johnny felt it utterly impossible to utter a word in reply.

"I'm afraid," pursued the seaman, closing the book, "that we've both had a bit too much of the savage about us—too much of the dancing round the fire. But mark me, Jack—we learn even in that book that a savage, a cannibal *may* be tamed; and we learn from something far better, that principle—the noblest principle which can govern either the young or the old—*may*, ay, and *must*, put out the fire of fierce anger in our hearts, and change us from wild beasts to men! So I've said my say," added Jonas with a smile, "and in token of my first victory over my old foe, come here, my boy, and give us your hand!"

"Oh, uncle, I am so sorry!" exclaimed Johnny, with moistened eyes, as he felt the kindly grasp of the old man.

"Sorry are you? and what were you on Saturday when I shook you as a cat shakes a rat?"

"Why, uncle, I own that I was angry."

"Sorry now, and angry then? So it's clear that the mild way has the best effect, to say nothing of the example." And Jonas fell into a fit of musing.

All was fair weather and sunshine in the home on that day, and on many days after. Jonas had, indeed, a hard struggle to subdue his temper, and often felt fierce anger rising in his heart, and ready to boil over in words of passion, or acts of violence; but Jonas, as he had endeavoured faithfully to serve his Queen, while he fought under her flag, brought the same earnest and brave sense of duty to bear on the trials of daily life. He never again forgot his resolution, and every day that passed made the restraint which he laid upon himself less painful and irksome to him.

If the conscience of any of my readers should tell him that, by his unruly temper, he is marring the peace of his family, oh! let him not neglect the evil as a small one, but, like the poor old sailor in my story, resolutely struggle against it. For *an angry man stirreth up strife, and a furious man aboundeth in transgression.*

There is sin in commencing strife;

Sin in the thoughtless jest

Or angry burst,

Which awakens first

The ire in a brother's breast!

There is sin in stirring up strife,

In fanning the smouldering flame,

By scornful eye,

Or proud reply,

Or anger-stirring name.

There is sin in keeping up strife,
Dark, soul-destroying sin.
Who cherishes hate
May seek heaven's gate,
But never can enter in.

For peace is the Christian's joy,
And love is the Christian's life;
He's bound for a home
Where hate cannot come,
Nor the shadow of sin or strife!

CHAPTER XII.
THE GIPSIES.

"If thou forbear to deliver them that are drawn unto death, and those that are ready to be slain; if thou sayest, Behold, we knew it not; doth not He that pondereth the heart consider it; and He that keepeth thy soul, doth He not know it? and shall not He render to every man according to his works?"—PROV. xxiv. 11, 12.

Alie sat on the threshold of her home on a bright morning in May, eating a cake which her uncle had given her, and now and then throwing a crumb to the merry little swallows that were twittering in the eaves and darting in and out of their nests.

Alie had not sat long when a tall, large-boned woman, in a red cloak, with sun-burnt features and wild dark eyes, approached her, followed by a miserable-looking little girl, about six or seven years of age, who had neither shoes on her blistered feet nor bonnet over her tangled hair. The gipsy stopped before Alie, and, in a tone which she intended to be winning, said, "Good mornin' to ye, my dear. Will ye cross my hand with silver, and I'll tell ye your fortin'?"

Alie promptly declined the offer, not only because she had been taught by her mother never to encourage those who pretend to be able to look into the future and to see what God has hidden from our eyes, but because the appearance of the woman frightened her. And had the gipsy said anything more to her, Alie would have retreated at once from the door. The woman, however, passed on, and a few yards further on found a willing listener in a flighty girl of the village, whose long gilt ear-rings, red ribands and curl-papers, were the outward tokens of such vanity and folly as might easily make her the dupe of a gipsy fortune-teller.

But the thin little girl lingered behind, shily eyeing Alie's tempting-looking cake. Alie broke off a piece and held it out to her. The child sidled up, took it, and devoured it as though she were famished. Alie smiled and gave her another bit.

"What is your name, little girl?" said Alie, first glancing to see that the gipsy was too much occupied to listen to her.

"Madge," answered the child.

"And is that woman your mother?"

Madge nodded her head in reply.

"And you go wandering about the country with her?"

Madge gave some low confused answer, which Alie could not at first understand; she made out from the child at last that the gipsy had pitched her tent somewhere near, and that she could not tell how long she would stay.

"Do you ever go to school, little Madge?"

The child only answered by a stare.

"Does any one teach you to read?"

Madge either did not comprehend the meaning of the question, or her eyes were wandering to Alie's white kitten, and she paid no attention to what was said. Alie marked the curious glance, and setting down her cake, went after her shy favourite, drew it from under the table where it had crouched, and carried it to the little girl at the door.

Alie's cake was nowhere to be seen, and the gipsy child was turning away!

"My cake!" exclaimed Alie. The girl started, and the piece of cake fell from her hand to the ground!

Alie, astonished as well as distressed, stood looking for a moment at the little culprit, then said in a voice of pity, "Pick it up, little Madge; you may eat it. I daresay that you are more hungry than I. But, oh!" she continued, as the child obeyed with an awkward air and a look of shame, "did you not know that it was very, very naughty to steal it? Did your mother never teach you that it is wrong to take what is not your own?"

ALIE AND THE GIPSY GIRL.

A strange expression stole over the face of the wretched girl, which, coupled with the gipsy woman's appearance and what Alie had heard of the character of some of the race, made her suspect that Madge would derive little benefit from her parent's instructions.

"Do you not know that God sees you?" pursued the young questioner.

"I know nothing about Him!" muttered the child.

"Not know about God!—never pray to Him!" exclaimed Alie.

But here the conversation was suddenly broken off by the gipsy woman calling to the child. Madge looked frightened, like one who had often found a word to be followed by a blow, and obeyed the call, though reluctantly, casting a parting look of regret, not at Alie, but at her pretty white kitten, and in a few minutes more both the gipsy and child had disappeared down a lane.

"Oh, poor, wretched little Madge!" thought Alie; "no wonder that she took the cake—no wonder if she grow up miserable and wicked! She does not know about God—she does not know that He made her—that He watches over her—that He hates sin, and will punish it! What will become of her in this world? what will become of her in the next?"

When her brother Johnny came home from the fields, Alie told him of the little gipsy girl.

"I've heard of the gipsies," said he; "they've pitched their tent down yon lane, and the farmer says that he must keep a good look-out after his poultry. There's a big woman, and an ill-looking man with a fur cap and a patch over his eye, who offers to mend kettles and pans. Farmer says he's sure the fellow has seen the inside of many a jail, and hopes the party won't stay long in the place."

THE GIPSIES.

"Poor little Madge! it's not her fault that she is the child of such people!" said Alie.

"She'll not get much good from them, I take it. She'll learn to tell falsehoods like her mother, and to steal like her father, and perhaps end her days in prison," observed Johnny.

Alie was silent for some time. Her fingers were now busily hemming a seam, but her thoughts were far away from her work. At last she said softly, as if to herself, "And yet that poor child is precious!"

"Precious to her parents! I don't believe it!" exclaimed Johnny. "She looks as though they half starved her; and didn't you see the bruises on her bare arms? I don't believe they'd care if she died in a ditch."

"She is precious in the eyes of the Lord," murmured Alie. "That poor little girl has a soul!"

Johnny did not answer for some time; and when he did so, it was with a forced lightness of manner. "I don't see what you and I have to do with the matter, Alie; we are not the little beggar's keepers!"

"*I am not my brother's keeper.* I have read these words somewhere in the Bible," said Alie; "but I can't at this moment remember what part of it they come from."

"Can't you?" replied Johnny; "why, they were the words of Cain, when he was asked about his brother Abel."

There was another long silence.

"I wonder," exclaimed Alie, clasping her hands, "if we could do nothing to save that poor child?"

"I can do nothing, at least," replied Johnny, and went whistling out of the house.

But Alie's mind was not so easily satisfied. She was one of those who have learned, from such solemn verses as that which stands at the commencement of my tale, that there is sin not only in doing the things which we ought not to do, but in *leaving undone* the things which we ought to do; and *doth not He that pondereth the heart consider it?* She knew that it is the duty, and ought to be the delight, of every Christian to help others on in the road to heaven, or lending good books, or assisting with the purse such valuable societies as have been formed to carry out this holy work.

Alie thought at first of watching for an opportunity when Madge might again pass the door, and giving to her a little copy of the "Young Cottager," which she had earned as a prize at school. But common sense (and common sense should always be taken into our council whenever we try to do good) showed her great objections to this. Madge could not read the book, nor understand it even if she could read. She was so ignorant, that whoever would teach her must begin with the very simplest form of instruction.

Alie dared not go to the gipsy tent: she was afraid of the woman, and yet more of the man; nor did she think that her mother would like her to visit those who bore such evil characters. Much did Alie wish that she could consult her mother, ever her best and wisest friend; but Mrs. Morris was at this time absent from home. Alie was not sufficiently at her ease with her uncle to speak to him on the subject; and as for her brother Johnny, he cared nothing at all about the matter.

Many children in Alie's place would have given up all idea of helping the gipsy girl, as a thing quite out of their power to do, and would have rested contented with the thought that this work was not intended for them. But Alie, timid and gentle as she was, was not one to be easily discouraged where her pity and her conscience were concerned. She remembered how the attention of Madge had been attracted by her pretty white kitten. Might not that kitten serve as a lure to draw the child a little way from the tent? There was a spot well known to Alie, where an old thorn-tree grew at the meeting of two lanes; it was about midway between the village and the place where the tent was pitched, and in sight of both. Alie thought that she might venture thus far, and seek to win an interview with the poor gipsy girl. There was one great difficulty in her way, at which the reader perhaps may smile: the old thorn could not be reached without passing the carrier's little yard, and the tenant of this yard was a large, fierce dog! True, the dog was chained; but Alie never felt as if iron or brass could stand the force of his sudden spring; and the sound of his low growl, and sharp, short bark, was to her terrible as the voice of a lion!

"Johnny," said Alie, "I wish that you would go a little way with me this evening; just as far as the thorn where the two roads meet."

"Do you want your fortune told, Alie?" replied Johnny, looking up with a saucy smile.

"No; but I wish to speak to little Madge, if you would only walk beside me so far."

"Oh, I wish you may get me!" exclaimed Johnny, chucking up a penny. "I'll have nothing to do with those beggarly gipsies!"

"If I go at all, I must go alone!" thought Alie; and alone she resolved to go! She saved a piece of bread from her own dinner, and wrapping up her white kitten in her checked apron, set out on her little expedition. She repeated to herself, as she walked, one of Watts' hymns for children, which, she thought, contained much truth in very small space, and might easily be both learned and remembered. The sound of it, too, was so pretty, that Madge could not dislike to learn that. Alie forgot all about the hymn, however, as she drew near the carrier's yard, and heard the rattle of a chain within. Almost as much afraid for her kitten as for herself, she pressed it closely to her bosom, and, going as near as she could to the opposite hedge, ran with a light, noiseless step past the spot; then paused to congratulate herself on the dreaded danger being over.

Alie reached the thorn in the lane, and to her pleasant surprise found Madge seated on the ground beneath it! The tent was at some little distance, though nearer than Alie liked to have it. A donkey was grazing beside it, and smoke was rising from a fire kindled of brushwood, over which a kettle was boiling.

I shall not dwell upon the conversation which passed between the two little girls. Alie found Madge more intelligent than she had expected; and the heart of the poor child, accustomed as she was to harshness and neglect, readily warmed towards one who seemed to take an interest in her welfare. Madge could not tell Alie how long the gipsies were likely to remain in that neighbourhood, but she eagerly agreed, as long as they stayed there, to meet her young friend every morning under the thorn.

The shadows were now growing long; the sun was sloping down to the west. A heavy step was heard along the lane, and a dark and ill-looking man approached, with a fur cap drawn low over his brow, and a stout crab-tree cudgel in his hand. Madge started to her feet like a frightened fawn, and, without a word of good-bye to her companion, started off for the tent. The man called after her in language which made Alie tremble, and it was the greatest relief to her when the gipsy had passed her without addressing or seeming to notice her. Again carefully wrapping up her kitten in her apron, Alie turned her face towards the village. As she proceeded along the lane, the distant sound of a sharp cry of pain coming from the direction of the tent, and then the angry tones of a man's voice, thrilled to her very soul. Full of sorrow and pity for another, Alie never even thought of the dog, till startled by a sudden bound and bark, which made her quicken her steps towards her home.

THE GIPSY'S APPROACH.

Madge was now almost constantly in the thoughts of Alie. To find some way of helping one so unhappy, of teaching one so ignorant, of pouring any sweetness into a cup so bitter, became the frequent occupation of her mind. Alie took pleasure in mending up old things and making new ones, reserving little dainties, contriving small surprises for the poor gipsy child in the lane. She searched out the most suitable verses to teach her, thought over improving stories to tell her, and never forgot, morning and night, to pray earnestly for the unhappy little girl.

And was all this trouble in vain? No; there was one lesson which poor Madge easily learned, and that was, to love her young teacher; and the next step was not a very hard one—to love that which she taught. It was glad tidings to the desolate girl to learn that there was a great and good Being who cared even for her; that there was a glorious crown prepared even for a gipsy child; that she who had never enjoyed the comfort of a home upon earth, might, after death, dwell in a bright home above the skies. Alie had not yet had many opportunities of serving God, or benefiting her fellow-creatures; but she had *done what she could.* She had sought out one wandering lamb; she had cheered one sorrowing heart; she had been a guide to one who had no other to win her from the way of misery and destruction. Oh! dear reader, could the same be said of you? *If thou forbear to deliver them that are drawn unto death, and those that are ready to be slain; if thou sayest, Behold, we knew it not; doth not He that pondereth the heart consider it? and He that keepeth thy soul, doth not He know it? and shall not He render to every man according to his works?*

Souls are perishing before thee—

Save, save one!

It may be thy crown of glory,—

Save, save one!

From the waves that would devour,

From the raging lion's power,

From destruction's fiery shower,

Save, save one!

Not in thine own strength confiding,

Save, save one!

Faith and prayer thy efforts guiding,

Save, save one!

None can e'er, unless possessing

Heavenly aid and heavenly blessing,

To the work of mercy pressing,

Save e'en one!

Who the worth of souls can measure?—

Save, save one!

Who can count the priceless treasure?

Save, save one!

Like the stars shall shine for ever

Those who faithfully endeavour

Dying sinners to deliver—

Save, save one!

CHAPTER XIII.
FRIENDS IN NEED.

"He that hath pity upon the poor lendeth unto the Lord; and that which he hath given will He pay him again."—PROV. xix. 17.

Alie went to the place of meeting early one morning, but Madge was not beneath the old thorn-tree. Alie did not hear the gipsy girl's accustomed greeting as she ran forward barefoot to meet her. Alie called her name softly, but no voice replied. She looked in the direction where the tent had been pitched; the tent was gone, there was nothing now to obstruct her view to the very end of the green lane! Alie felt sad, and yet thankful. What a short time had been given to her in which she could serve poor Madge! But that short time had not been wasted; she had caught the opportunity on the wing, before, as she believed, it had passed away for ever.

"But I should have liked to have seen her once more. I should have liked to have said 'good-bye,' and to have given her something to keep as a remembrance of me," thought Alie, as she slowly walked along the lane towards the blackened spot which showed where the gipsies had lighted their fire.—"Perhaps we shall never look on each other's faces again, until we meet before the great white throne. Oh! may we both be on the right hand then. She *did* love to listen when I told her of the Lord; and He can keep her from temptation, and guide her to Himself. She promised to repeat, morn and night, that little prayer which I taught her. I think that she will do so, if only for my sake; for I am sure that she loved me—poor unhappy little Madge. Oh! if I had had time to teach her a few verses more."

THE GREEN LANE.

Alie was startled from her reflections by a sound something between a sob and a cry, which came from some place near the spot where the tent of the gipsies had stood. She stopped, listened, and heard it again. The voice was like that of one in bitter distress. Alie fancied that she could distinguish her own name! Doubtless it was poor Madge who was crying; but if she were there, so might her parents be also, and Alie was terrified at the idea of meeting the gipsies in so lonely a spot, quite out of sight of any dwelling. She could see nothing of them as she looked down the lane: but again and again rose that wailing cry.

"It is that *fear of man* which would keep me now from doing to others as I would they should do unto me," thought Alie; and, mustering all her resolution, she ventured further into the lane. She had not proceeded many steps when she heard the voice of Madge distinctly exclaim, in tones of tremulous joy, "Oh! it is you, Alie! it is you at last! I thought that you would come to the thorn; but, oh, I was so afraid that you would not hear my crying—that you would go away, and leave me here to starve!"

"Where are you?" exclaimed Alie, looking about her in surprise at not seeing the speaker.

"Here—up here, just at the other side of the hedge."

"Why don't you come down?"

"I can't—I'm tied to a tree! I've been tied all night!" exclaimed the poor child, bursting into an agony of tears, which for some time prevented Alie from understanding another word which she uttered.

Alie lost no time in making her way to the place. She clambered up the mossy bank, careless of nettles—scrambled over the low briery hedge on the top—and beyond it, fastened to the trunk of a tree she found the unhappy Madge, pale, exhausted with crying and want of rest, her arms chafed by the cord which bound her, and which she had vainly struggled to break. Happily Alie had a knife in her pocket, or she could never have unloosed the tightened knots. The moment that Madge was free, she fell sobbing into the arms of her deliverer.

"How cruel! oh, how cruel to bind you so!" exclaimed Alie; "what had you done to make them so angry?"

"I had done nothing!" cried Madge between her sobs. "Perhaps they wanted to keep me from going after them: they need not have been afraid—I'd have given no trouble!"

"Do you think that they mean to come back soon?" said Alie, glancing timidly around.

"I don't think so," replied the girl. "They would not tell me where they were going, nor let me see which way they went. It was all done so quick! Father came home late yesterday, and said something to mother—something about being found out; mother started, seemed afraid, and pointed to me. Then they whispered together—looking at me every minute; and then they pulled down the tent, and packed up all in haste; and before they left, father tied me up here, and said he'd beat me if I made any noise."

"Let's come to my home," said Alie, "and ask mother what's to be done. You must want a little breakfast sadly, and a little rest too, poor, poor Madge!"

Before many minutes were over the gipsy girl was seated at Mrs. Morris's deal table with a basin of warm bread and milk before her, feeling something like a traveller after a stormy voyage, when he has cast anchor in a haven at last. When Madge's hunger was satisfied, Alie led her to her own little crib, where the poor child soon fell into a refreshing sleep.

Great was the wrath, great the indignation of Jonas, the old sailor, when, on returning from his morning stroll, he heard from his sister the story of Madge. The idea of a helpless and innocent child being thus maltreated and abandoned, roused all the lion in his soul. Down came his brown fist with startling violence on the table—as with hearty good-will he might have laid it on the gipsy; and a torrent of fierce abuse was about to pour from his lips, when, recollecting his resolution, he pressed them together with a mighty effort, and suffered his indignation to escape only through his flashing eyes.

"It is evident," said Mrs. Morris, "that they have found the poor child a burden, and so, hoping that she has made friends in this village, they have gone off and left her, taking care that no one should be able to trace them."

"They are—" commenced the sailor fiercely, then closed his lips tightly again.

"And now," continued Mrs. Morris, "the difficulty is how to dispose of this poor child. Notwithstanding all my efforts, I find it no easy matter in these hard times to maintain my own family, and send Johnny and Alie to school. I do not see how it would be possible for me to undertake the support of another child."

"Then, mother," said Johnny, who was present, "what will you do with poor Madge?"

"I do not see what I can do," replied his mother, "but send her at once to the workhouse."

"The workhouse!" exclaimed Johnny.

"The workhouse!" echoed Alie. "Oh, mother, I'd work my fingers to the bone rather than send poor Madge away! She can share my dinner, my breakfast, my bed."

Mrs. Morris gravely shook her head; but Alie was too earnest to be easily discouraged.

"I could earn something—I really could, mother! You know that Mrs. Mant said that I might help her in mending!" and the little girl looked imploringly into the face of her mother.

"My dear child, what you could earn would not supply Madge with enough of food to keep life in."

"I could get something for chopping firewood," began Johnny, and then stopped short; "but I hate the trouble, and shouldn't much like to tie myself up to do it! 'Twouldn't do to begin and not go on, I take it."

"It wouldn't do at all," replied Mrs. Morris.

Jonas sat in profound thought, appearing as though he were making some deep calculation on his fingers. The truth is that the old seaman had as warm a heart and as strong a desire to help the outcast as any one present; but his means of doing so were very small. Much the greater part of his little pension was regularly paid to his sister, to cover the necessary expenses of the sailor's board and lodging; and what Jonas reserved for himself was such a mere trifle that it barely sufficed to supply him with clothing, and replenish his little tobacco pouch. But he, like Alie, was disposed to regard the desolate stranger as one whom the Almighty had committed to their protection, and the idea of sending her away to the workhouse was repugnant to his kindly nature. Jonas turned over and over in his mind the means of supporting the child until she should be able to do something for herself, and at length he came to a decision.

"Yes," he muttered half to himself, "yes, that's the thing! 'Twill cost me something maybe at first; but it's right, and I'll do it! The gipsy lass shall have my pipe!"

The children could not forbear laughing. "Little use she could make of it!" cried Johnny.

"That's the way with you younkers," said Jonas rather pettishly; "you never know how to put two and two together. What's a pipe without 'bacco, and how's 'bacco to be had without money?" he continued, raising his voice;—"the money that buys 'bacco for me would buy bread for the gipsy; and your little earnings, my lass," he added, turning to Alie, "put on the top of my savings, might serve to keep the little boat afloat, without running it on the rough shore of a workhouse."

Alie clapped her hands in delight. The eye of Mrs. Morris glistened. "My dear brother," said she, "I won't be behind you in this labour of love. If you think of making such a sacrifice—"

"Think!" cried Jonas bluffly, "it's not thinking, but doing!" and, stumping up to the fireplace with an air of resolution, he again took his pipe from its place and deliberately snapped it in two! but could not refrain from a sigh as he looked on the broken pieces.

"You need not have broken it," observed Johnny; "'twould have done no mischief where it was."

"'Twould have been a temptation," replied Jonas, rubbing his chin; "'twould ha' been always putting me in mind of a want. If I hadn't broke my pipe, maybe I'd ha' broke my resolution."

"You will miss it sadly, I fear," said Mrs. Morris.

How much the poor old sailor missed his accustomed indulgence can only be guessed by those who have, like him, formed a habit of smoking till the pipe seems as necessary as daily food. It is a habit which I hope that none of my young readers will adopt; the expense of it being one of its least disadvantages. But Jonas had been accustomed to smoke from his youth; he looked to his pipe as to his comfort and companion, and, in giving it up, he sacrificed really more than a lady would in putting down her carriage, or a sportsman in selling off his hounds. Therefore his pence were a nobler offering than their hundreds of guineas would have been.

Madge was now the happy inmate of a home, whose simple comforts appeared luxuries to her. Its inmates vied with each other in showing her kindness. Except in school-time, or when she was at meals, Alie's little hands were busy from morning till night; and even Johnny tried his skill in cobbling a very old pair of his sister's shoes for Madge, and succeeded, more to his own admiration, it must be owned, than to that of any one else. Madge was now made neat and clean, her hair cut and brushed, her rags mended; and the change in her appearance was so great that Jonas said, looking at her with quiet satisfaction, that "he should not ha' known the lass." There was a bright, happy expression now in Madge's blue eyes, and she did not start when suddenly addressed, as if she were afraid of being struck.

And if the outward change was so great, there was every probability that the inward would be yet more striking. Madge was docile and willing to be taught, and she could not be long under the roof of Mrs. Morris without receiving knowledge of the best and highest kind. The distinctions between right and wrong, truth and falsehood, honesty and theft, were becoming daily more and more clear to the child; and she was gradually learning that which would give her the strongest motive for refusing the evil and choosing the good.

Madge had not been many days in her new home, when, to the surprise of the little family, then assembled round the dinner-table, a post-chaise stopped at the entrance. A gentleman dressed in black, with a paper in his hand, descended from the vehicle, and, after tapping at the door, though it stood open on account of the heat of the weather, walked straight into the kitchen.

"Beg pardon—pray don't move," said he, waving his hand slightly, as the family rose at his entrance. "May I ask if your name is Morris?" he continued, first glancing at his paper, then at Alie's mother.

Wondering, and half alarmed at the unexpected visit, Mrs. Morris only answered by dropping a little courtesy; while Jonas muttered something about "land-shark," which it was intended no one should hear.

"I thought so—hum!" said the lawyer, for such he was. "I have been directed to you as one who might give me some information as to the movements of a party of gipsies, upon whose track I have been for the last ten days."

"Indeed, sir, I know little about them," replied Mrs. Morris. "Some gipsies were in this neighbourhood about a week ago."

"But they made all sail last Thursday night," joined in the sailor.

"A tall woman, and a man with a patch over his eye," said the lawyer, examining his paper.

"That's 'em," cried Jonas; "an ill-looking pair, and a sight worse than they look."

"Can you tell me in which direction they went?" said the stranger, addressing himself to the sailor.

"Not I, sir," replied honest Jonas.

"They have a child with them, have they not—a little girl?"

"They had a child, sir, but they tied her up like a dog, and left her behind when they made off."

"Ha!" exclaimed the lawyer eagerly; "and have you any knowledge where she may be now?"

"I should think that I have, seeing she's just alongside," cried Jonas, looking round for poor Madge, who, alarmed at finding herself the subject of conversation, had slunk behind her little friend Alie.

All the lawyer's attention was now turned towards Madge. He fixed his piercing gaze upon the timid child, questioned and cross-questioned her without mercy, not only about events which had happened recently, but, as it appeared to Johnny and Alie, about everything that could possibly have occurred in the whole course of a gipsy's life. The dinner on the table was becoming quite cold; but the stranger had as little apparent regard for the hunger of the family as he had for the feelings of Madge. He wrote down most of the replies which he drew from her shy, reluctant lips, and concluded by proposing that she should accompany him in the post-chaise, as there was very important business connected with the child.

This was too much for poor Madge. She clung tightly to Alie, and, bursting into tears, begged that she might not be sent away.

"But if I were to take you to a fine house and fine friends, my dear?" said the lawyer, in an insinuating tone. "I may tell you that you were not born a gipsy; nor were those who deserted you your real parents. You were stolen long ago by those who have passed you off as their child. Your mother, Mrs. Everard, has been anxiously searching after you for years, and joyful indeed will she be to find that our search has at last been successful."

Alie and Johnny gave exclamations of pleasure and surprise, Jonas was startled into uttering a whistle, but Madge scarcely understood the good news—she still clung to her early friend, and sobbed out that she didn't want to go away, she wouldn't go away with that man!

"Well," said the lawyer, with a smile, after a few vain attempts to coax her into confidence, "it is evident that she is both safe and contented where she now is. Let her remain here for the present, till her mother can come herself and claim her stray lamb from those who have so hospitably afforded her shelter and protection."

It would be difficult to describe all the talking, wondering, guessing, which went on in Mrs. Morris's dwelling after the lawyer had driven from her door. The news spread like wild-fire through the village; all kinds of additions were made to a story in itself sufficiently strange; and the kitchen was soon filled to overflowing with neighbours eager for news. Before night came, the patience of Jonas was fairly tired out by insatiable questioners; and his pipe, had he still possessed one, would have been in imminent peril. The person who appeared least excited and delighted was poor little Madge herself, who would rather have been told that she might remain with Alie and her mother to the end of her days, than that she was to live in a palace and be the daughter of a queen. She was like a weary, wounded bird, that has found a peaceful nest; and she was too young and ignorant to understand all the reasons that might make it an advantage to her to quit it for another.

But Madge was a very happy girl the next day, when she found herself in the arms of a mother—a *real* mother—one who, with love and joy streaming from her eyes, pressed her long lost darling close and closer to her heart, as though she would hold her there for ever. With feelings of natural delicacy, Mrs. Morris and her family retired to Jonas's little room, and closed the door, not to intrude by their presence on the intense joy of a parent at such a meeting. What the lady said to Madge, or Madge to the lady, they therefore never knew; but what account the child had given of the generous kindness of her friends was easily to be seen when, at her mother's desire, she called them to speak to her. Mrs. Everard grasped the hand of Mrs. Morris with deep emotion; thanked her with tears in her eyes; and insisted on her accepting from her, as an acknowledgment of her debt, a sum which would have covered poor Madge's expenses for years! The lady had brought her carriage half full of presents for the children; beautiful books, choice sweetmeats and cakes—never before had the plain deal table been loaded with such a heap of good things! Alie found herself dressed from head to foot in nicer clothes than she ever had worn; for Madge insisted on her putting them on at once, that she might see how Alie looked in them, and laughed and clapped her hands with delight, as though this were to her the greatest treat of all. Johnny felt almost ashamed to accept the numerous presents; he felt that he had so little deserved them—he had done so little, sacrificed so little, to promote the comfort of the stranger.

Suddenly a thought seemed to cross the mind of Madge, which cast a momentary shade over her bright little face. She ran up to her mother, laid hold on her arm with childish eagerness, and, pointing to old Jonas, who was looking with hearty enjoyment on the scene before him, exclaimed in an audible whisper, "Have you brought nothing for him?"

"Blessings on the lass!" cried the honest sailor; "I want nothing but such a sight as this! 'Tis as good as the view of the old white cliffs to the homeward-bound!"

"He was so kind—so very kind," continued Madge, without noticing the interruption; "he broke his pipe, and gave up all his smoking, that I might not be sent to the workhouse. Alie told me he did, and Alie always says true; and he ought to have some of the cake."

The conclusion of Madge's speech set all the party laughing—Jonas laughing the loudest of all. Mrs. Everard put her arm fondly around her little girl. "Perhaps we could think of something that our good friend would like still better than cake," she said, gently.

Madge looked wistfully at Alie, her usual counsellor as well as friend. Suddenly her face brightened. "I know! I know!" she exclaimed; "I once heard him say he wished he'd a glass like those on board a ship, and he'd show us the hills a long way off, and the mountains in the moon beside."

"A telescope he shall have," said Mrs. Everard, "and one of the best that can be made."

The lady was as good as her word, and the sailor the next day became the happy owner of that which it had long been his wish to possess, though that such a wish should ever be gratified had never entered into the good man's calculations.

"It seems so strange," whispered Alie to Madge, "so very strange, that we should be so thanked and rewarded for such little acts of kindness. I don't believe that such a thing ever happened before."

"My child, you are mistaken," said Mrs. Everard, who chanced to hear the observation; "more wondrous things are happening every day—things of which the present scene is like a type. The poorest, weakest little one who suffers on earth, and needs the hand of Christian kindness, is the child of a Parent infinitely rich, infinitely great, who deigns to notice, and who will a thousand-fold reward, the smallest kindness shown for His sake. Nothing given in charity is ever lost; no effort made for charity is ever forgotten. *Inasmuch as ye did it unto the least of these My brethren, ye did it unto Me*, are the words of Him who holds in His hands all the treasures of earth and heaven. We may not, perhaps, see in this world—but assuredly we shall see in the next—that however worthless in themselves our services may be, the Almighty condescends to accept them; and that, *he that hath pity upon the poor lendeth unto the Lord, and that which he hath given will He pay him again*."

Help the poor who need your aid,

Help with silver and with gold.

Ye whom God hath stewards made.

In your hands His wealth to hold.

Help the poor by kindly deed;

Hands in willing service move,

Clothe the bare, the hungry feed,

Weary ne'er in acts of love.

Help the poor by kindly word;

Comfort, counsel, wisely given,

Such by wandering sinners heard.

May those sinners lead to heaven.

Help the poor by earnest prayer—

Lift your heart unto the Lord;

He alone can bless your care,

Make success its rich reward.

Gifts, words, works, and prayers shall yet

Bring the Christian harvest sure;

God will not your love forget:

Blessed he that helps the poor.

CHAPTER XIV.
THE OLD PAUPER.

"The foolishness of man perverteth his way; and his heart fretteth against the Lord."—PROV. xix. 3.

"It is very very hard in one's old age to be driven to poverty, to be neglected by one's friends, forsaken by one's children—left to wear out a weary life in a hateful place like this!"

Such were the words of a miserable old man, who, bedridden and helpless, was pouring out his complaint to a humane visitor at the workhouse.

"But, my friend," replied the lady, "we must remember that these trials are sent by a gracious and merciful God, who *does not afflict willingly, nor grieve the children of men.*"

THE OLD PAUPER.

"It's all very well for those to talk who don't know what trouble means," said old Sam Butler, in a tone of peevish irritability. "Where is the mercy shown to me? I was once a strong, hearty young man—none better at cricket or at football; and now I can't so much as creep across this hateful room! I had once my own well-stocked shop, with the customers thronging in and out like bees; and now, but for the workhouse, I shouldn't have a roof over my head! I was once surrounded by a wife and children—a thriving, goodly family; and now my wife's in her grave, and the children scattered over the world, and there's not one of them that so much as cares to inquire whether the old man's dead or alive! Oh! it's very hard! it's very very hard!"

"But there are some comforts and hopes of which neither old age nor sickness, neither man's neglect nor poverty can ever deprive us."

"Don't talk to me!" cried the old pauper, angrily. "I know all that you're going to say, but there's neither comfort nor hope to me in these things. I never found any in my better days, and I'm not likely to find any now!"

The visitor looked shocked and distressed. She felt anxious to speak a message of peace to the wretched old man; but his bitterness of spirit and rebellion of will made her find it difficult to address him. Thinking that to reflect on the trials of others might divert his mind from his own, or give him an indirect lesson on resignation under them, she said, after a few moments' hesitation, "I have recently been visiting one who has known much affliction—a poor man of the name of Charles Hayes—"

"Charles Hayes!" interrupted the pauper; "as if I did not know him!—my schoolfellow when I was a boy, and my neighbour for twenty long years! I always said he would come to the workhouse—what with his bad health and his silly scruples about turning an honest penny; thinking everything wrong which did not square with his odd notions, and helping others when he had scarcely enough for himself! I always said he would come to the workhouse. And yet, see what a world this is!" continued Butler with a burst of indignation; "no sooner is he quite laid on the shelf than the gentry take to petting and pampering him as if he were one of themselves! The squire gets him into an alms-house, the ladies send him blankets and broth, the parson takes a pleasure in visiting him, and he is watched day and night with as much care as if he were one of the lords of the land!"

"Watched by an orphan whom he had generously brought up."

"Other people have brought up children," cried the pauper, with something like a groan, "and have had no comfort in them. Charles Hayes had never a child of his own, but he finds one like a daughter by his sick-bed; he has always been poor, but now in his age I don't believe that he wants for anything—a friend seems to meet him wherever he turns; and they say that in spite of his weakness and pain he calls himself contented and happy! Oh! this is a bad world!—a miserable world! Why should his lot be so different from mine? Why should he have peace, and I have nothing but trouble? Why should his friends stick by him, and all mine forsake me? Why, when I am wearing out my days in a workhouse, should he rest in a home of his own?"

An answer was on the visitor's lips, but consideration for the feelings of the pauper prevented her from uttering it aloud—"Because *the blessing of the*

Lord it maketh rich, and He addeth no sorrow therewith." There would have been no use in attempting to point out to the repining old man how godliness, even in this world, brings its reward; nor did the lady know enough of the events of Butler's life to be aware how completely his present miseries were the natural consequences of his own conduct. Self had ever been his first object; to gratify self had been the business of his life. He had not served God in the time of his health; he could not look to God in the hour of his helplessness and need. He had done nothing to benefit man, and man cared nothing for him now, though compassion might bring a few, like the visitor at the workhouse, to spend some minutes beside him as a disagreeable duty.

Yet Sam Butler had set out in life with no bad prospects. Blessed with cheerful spirits, buoyant health, a fair education and good name, and settled in a comfortable situation, he seemed likely to do well in the world, and spend a very prosperous life.

The first great mistake which Butler made was that of marrying for money. His master was old and infirm, and willing to give up his business whenever his only daughter should marry one able to assist her in carrying it on. Betsy was neither pleasing in person nor agreeable in manner. She was proud, passionate, and self-willed, with a heart utterly worldly, in which piety had never found a place. Sam cared nothing for her, but he cared much for the shop; and, regardless of the command to marry *only in the Lord*, he vowed to love and cherish until death a woman whom he secretly despised. Degraded in his own eyes by his worldly marriage, Butler was not long in discovering that he had sold his happiness for gold. The comfort of a cheerful, peaceful home, was never to be his. Whenever he crossed his own threshold, the first sound which struck his ears was the voice of peevishness and ill-temper. What wonder if he often passed his evenings at places which it would have been better for him if he had never entered, and sought elsewhere for that enjoyment which by his own hearth he never could find!

At this time Charles Hayes was the near neighbour of Sam Butler. He was united to one who, like himself, was serving God with a humble heart, and a cheerful, contented spirit. If Charles's home was lowly, it was peaceful; if he had little of this world's goods, he had few of its cares: labour and poverty might be his lot, but piety and love sweetened all.

But affliction, from which even the most faithful servants of God are not exempted, was sent to the cottage of Charles Hayes. His beloved partner was suddenly called to her rest. Sore was the trial to the Christian, when he stood by the grave of the young wife who had been dearer to him than all the world beside, and who was worthy of all his affection. But his was a sorrow *not without hope*. He looked forward, even when grief bowed his heart to the dust, to a blessed reunion in a land where parting shall never be known; though divided from his wife by death, he could think of her as "not lost, but gone before;" and when time had mellowed the sharpness of his pain, there was no earthly pleasure for which he would have exchanged the sweet remembrance of years spent in happiness with one who was now an angel in heaven!

Sam Butler had a family, and, as he would proudly say, there were no children in all the village so healthy and handsome as his own. He was by no means wanting in parental affection; and it was a pleasing sight to see him in the evening, when the day's business was over, with one laughing little one perched on his shoulder, and another holding fast to his hand, chasing the third down a daisy-mottled slope, while the neighbourhood rang with the sound of their mirth. Sam made great projects for his children, and built for them castles in the air without end. Patrick was to get a grand education—perhaps go to the bar, distinguish himself by his talents, and rise to the highest honours. "We'll see you Chancellor yet!" the proud father would cry, clapping his boy on the back, when the little fellow, who was sharp and ready of wit, had said something more flippant than usual.

Dan, according to Butler's plans, should keep the shop—make money with wonderful success—go to London, and in time become an alderman—feast upon turtle, entertain princes, and perhaps end by being elected Lord Mayor! As for Nina, his beautiful little Nina, Butler had still wilder speculations for her.

But there was one thing which Butler had left out of all his calculations. He never remembered that "man proposes, but God disposes;" and that the blessing of the Almighty alone could make his children either prosperous or happy. He neglected to *train up his children in the way in which they should go*; or rather, he himself led his children in the way in which they should *not* go; and when old, they did not depart from it.

Charles Hayes came to Butler one day, drawing along with him, by a firm grasp on the shoulder, the half-resisting, terrified Patrick, who, with lips blackened with cherries, and pockets dropping gooseberries, stood before his father the picture of a self-convicted thief.

"I am very sorry to say," began Charles, "that I have found your boy in my garden, and, I fear, not for the first time. I thought it best to bring him at once to his father, that he may receive from you such a punishment as may make him a better and more honest boy."

"Well," said Butler, carelessly, "I'm sorry he has done mischief in your garden, neighbour; but it's the nature of boys to love fruit. We must remember that we were children once."

"It is not the fruit that I care for," said Charles; "but it grieves me to see the sin. Every river was a brook once, every oak an acorn; and the boy who steals unheeded a cherry from a tree may end his days in prison as a thief!"

Sam chucked his boy under the chin, told him to mind what he had heard, and turned away with some jesting remark about the ease with which those who have no children of their own can manage the children of others.

"*He that spareth the rod hateth his son,*" thought Charles Hayes, as he slowly returned to his cottage.

Butler's shop was one in which a variety of cakes and sweetmeats were sold, and he invariably kept it open on Sundays. "I make more on that day than on any other day in the week," he used to say. "No one but a fool would beggar himself for the sake of idle scruples I keep my conscience in my till!"

Butler's shop was, indeed, more full than usual on that day which we have been commanded to *keep holy*. And did he benefit by disobedience? He certainly thought that he did. His Nina dressed more gaily, his own table was better supplied, his boys had more sports, he was enabled himself to drink deeper, than if, like his neighbour, he had devoted his Sabbaths to rest and religion. But was he really the better for his unhallowed gains?—were his wife or his children the better? Oh, no! the example which he set, the company which he kept, were surely and not slowly corrupting and destroying the source of even his earthly happiness. We have read of a Spanish general who was so fond of money that the enemies into whose hands he had fallen tortured and killed him by pouring melted gold down his throat, in mockery of his covetousness! So Satan now often makes money unlawfully acquired the very means of tormenting the miserable beings who have sold their conscience to obtain it. There is no blessing on it, no blessing can be expected with it, and it is not only at the judgment-day that ill-gotten wealth shall crush its owner beneath its weight!

Butler had gradually acquired in the taverns, to which he had been driven by the temper of his wife, a taste for spirituous liquors. He was what is called "a jovial fellow;" and if his Sunday mornings were spent in business, his Sunday evenings were spent in revels. He was fond of placing his little Dan on the table, and calling for a song from the child; and then, when the boy had set all present in a roar of laughter by his fun, would reward him by giving him a sip from the brimming glass which he himself loved too well. Poor boy! it had been better for him if it had been poison that passed his lips!

Nina, too, was brought forward to be admired and flattered by her father's Sunday guests, and to have the seeds of folly and vanity planted in a soil which was but too ready to receive them.

While Butler's children were yet young, their mother died. Her death was little regretted by her husband; and yet it proved to him no small misfortune. Her temper had made his home uncomfortable, but she had preserved in it something like order and regularity. She had had some influence over her children; and though she had never used it to implant in their young minds those principles which might have survived herself, and guided them to virtue and happiness, yet that influence had been some restraint, at least, on their outward conduct. Now all curb upon them was taken away. They became each year more ungovernable and wild; their extravagance emptied the purse of their father much faster than his gains could fill it. If the sin of Sabbath-breaking made money seem to flow readily into it, other sins, to which Sabbath-breaking gave rise, made holes for that money to flow through. Butler became a poorer and poorer man. He drank more, to drown thought, and so hastened the ruin which he dreaded. He became so irregular in his habits that all respectable customers gave him up. Companions he had still, but friends he had none. He had trifled with his health, now it failed him; and neither of his sons, though intelligent youths, were sufficiently steady and regular to be fitted to take his place in the shop. Butler fell, gradually fell, from one stage of ruin to another. He saw all his comforts one by one disappear. A blight, a mildew was upon his fair hopes; a worm was at the root of his joys. He lived to see his daughter, once his pride, make a silly marriage, without his consent, to a worthless, dissipated soldier, who carried her away to a distant land, where her father never heard of her more. He lived to see his boys grow up unprincipled men, undutiful sons,—the one a drunkard, the other a thief! He lived to see his home in the hands of a stranger, and to be himself, in his old age, compelled to seek the dreary shelter of a workhouse.

Bitterly Butler murmured against the decrees of Providence, which he believed had brought him to misery. Bitterly he complained of poverty and desertion, and the feebleness of a broken constitution. And yet he was but reaping as he had sowed! Self-indulgence, self-will, self-worship, were but bearing their natural fruit; and what Butler called his misfortunes were but the first instalment of the miserable *wages of sin. The foolishness of man perverteth his way; and his heart fretteth against the Lord.*

There are no chains that bind

So close as chains of sin;
There are no foes we find
So stern as foes within.
God may send pain and loss
To those whom most He loves;
But heavier far than such a cross
The sinner's burden proves!

'Tis guilt that barbs the dart,
'Tis guilt that binds the cord;
Yet the deceiving heart
Will fret against the Lord!
When mirth in anguish ends,
Man dreads the truth to own
That from the Lord all good descends,
Despair from sin alone!

CHAPTER XV.
THE BEAUTIFUL VILLA.

"Favour is deceitful, and beauty is vain: but a woman that feareth the Lord, she shall be praised."—PROV. xxxi. 20.

Jessy Warner stood before a pier-glass, gazing on the image reflected in it with silent delight. And truly the image was a very pretty one, though perhaps not all the world would have admired it as much as the vain young lady. She had twined a wreath of flowers in her luxuriant tresses, and smoothed every ringlet till it lay on her fair neck bright as burnished gold. She was smiling at the form in the mirror, which smiled again, displaying an even row of pearly teeth; and Jessy was evidently too much charmed with her occupation to give a thought to the pile of lesson-books which lay unopened on the table, or the unfinished jacket beside it, which her lazy little fingers had failed in a whole month to complete.

Mrs. Warner entered unobserved by Jessy, and that which made the young daughter smile cost the mother a sigh.

"My poor child is so much engaged in contemplating her own pretty face, that everything else is neglected and forgotten!" Such were the reflections of Mrs. Warner. "Oh, how shall I teach her the comparative worthlessness of that which is only skin-deep—that which time must impair, and any hour may destroy!"

She moved forward a few steps, and her reflection in the glass first made Jessy aware of her presence.

"Oh, mamma!" she exclaimed, "I did not know that you were there;" and a blush rose to Jessy's cheek at being discovered in the act of admiring her own beauty. Mrs. Warner glanced at the books and the work, but made no observation on the subject; and merely asked her daughter if she were inclined for a walk, and would like to accompany her to a house at some distance, where she was about to pay a visit on business.

"I should like it of all things," cried Jessy, hastily divesting her head of its gay wreath—so hastily that many of the flower-petals were strewed on the floor.

"These were very bright and beautiful to-day—what will they be to-morrow?" observed the lady.

Jessy made no reply, but hastened to put on her bonnet and shawl.

Mrs. Warner gave her daughter an allowance for her dress; Jessy was therefore able to choose it herself, and please her own taste in the selection.

It must be owned that her attire was more remarkable for the gaiety of its colours than for the goodness of its materials—that more attention was paid to its being becoming than to its being comfortable; and that money was often wasted upon some expensive piece of finery, when some necessary article of dress was required. Jessy's bonnet was now radiant with pink bows and flowers, and pretty bracelets adorned her arms; while her gloves were so old that the fingers looked through them, and her shoes were so much trodden down at heel that she could not help shuffling as she walked. Jessy was in actual want of a good common dress, in which she could run about the garden, and play with her young companions without fear of causing rent or stain; but she had chosen one of a tint so delicate, and a fabric so fragile, that she never, while wearing it, felt at her ease.

Mrs. Warner and her daughter pursued their way along green shady lanes, and across daisy-dotted meadows, with nothing to mar the pleasure of their walk, except the brambles in the former, which were always catching in poor Jessy's flounces, and the stiles in the latter, which her tight dress made her find difficulty in crossing. Jessy and her mother arrived at last at an exceedingly beautiful spot. On an emerald lawn, embosomed in trees, stood a villa which might have been the abode of a fairy, so tasteful was its form, so graceful its fanciful minarets, so elegant its windows of stained glass overhung with clusters of roses and jasmine. A splendid passion-flower twined round one of the slender carved pillars of the porch; another was half hidden by clematis. In the centre of the building rose an ornamental clock-tower, whose gilded pinnacle glittered in the sun! In her admiration of its fanciful beauty, Jessy did not notice that the hands of the gay clock pointed to a wrong hour, for its works were motionless and out of order.

MRS. WARNER AND JESSY.

"Oh," she exclaimed, "what a lovely place! How delightful it would be to live here! How proud one would be if it were one's own!"

"It is pretty enough on the outside," said Mrs. Warner, rather drily; "but with houses, as with those who live in them, it is not sufficient to look only at the *face*—we must examine further before we decide whether they are subjects either for pride or for admiration."

They entered the pretty porch, and Mrs. Warner pulled the bell-handle. It was broken, and came off in her hand; so, seeing that the door was open, the lady walked into the house.

Strangely different from what the exterior had led her to expect, Jessy found the inside of the dwelling. It bore every token of neglect and disrepair, as if either uninhabited or occupied by those who paid no attention to neatness and comfort. The plaster had partly peeled from the walls; there was not a carpet upon the floors, and the dust lay so thick upon them that the visitors' footsteps left prints behind! There was a sad lack of chairs and tables, even of the commonest kind, in the sitting-room, which Mrs. Warner entered in hopes of finding a more efficient bell. Jessy sat down on a bench, and had a narrow escape of falling to the ground, for one of the legs gave way beneath even her light weight!

"What a shame to furnish such a pretty house so badly!" she exclaimed. "I never saw a place so neglected! Just look at the dull spotted picture-frames, and the dirty cobwebs across the corners of the room! What is the use of having a beautiful house, if nothing but rubbish is in it?"

"What is the use, indeed!" replied Mrs. Warner, trying again the effect of pulling the old bell-rope. "But houses are not the only things which need furnishing; and yet I fancy that there is some one not far from me who occasionally acts as though she thought that it matters not how empty a head may be, so that it looks well to the eye."

"Oh, mamma!" cried Jessy laughing, yet half vexed, "heads and houses are such different things!"

"To my idea," replied Mrs. Warner, "an unfurnished mind is much like an unfurnished house, only a much sadder object. Youth is the time above all other to fit up the intellect richly. We may then lay in an almost boundless store of valuable information, increasing with every day of our lives, for none are too old to learn."

"But study is so tiresome!" sighed Jessy.

"It costs us something, my dear; like rich furniture, it is not to be had for the mere wishing. But it is well worth the trouble which it costs. And remember, Jessy, with the mind, as with the house, it cannot be *entirely* empty. Where knowledge is neglected folly will come—the dust gathers, the spider spins her web. If we are not learning we are losing—a mind left to itself is a mind left to decay!"

"I wonder if any one lives here!" said Jessy, who was rather desirous to turn the conversation. "No one takes the trouble to answer the bell."

"I believe that we shall find Madame L'Ame in one of the upper rooms," replied her mother. "She knows me well, and therefore will not regard my visit as an intrusion; besides, to-day she expects me, as I have to speak to her on important business, regarding a large property to which she is heir."

Mrs. Warner, therefore, followed by her daughter, proceeded up the dusty uncarpeted stair, Jessy feeling some curiosity to see the mistress of the beautiful but neglected mansion. They reached the landing-place, where Mrs. Warner knocked at the door of one of the upper rooms. As the sound brought no answer, the lady knocked again, when a shrill voice bade her "come in;" and she and Jessy entered an apartment as unsightly as the rest of the interior of the house. There was not, perhaps, the same deficiency of furniture, but everything was in confusion and disorder, as it might be heaped together in the warehouse of a broker. At one corner of the room a maidservant on her knees was engaged in cutting out pictures from old magazines of fashion, figures of slender-waisted belles and coxcomicallooking beaux, and pasting them on a large screen. This Jessy observed when she had a little leisure to look around her, but at first her attention was engaged by the mistress of the house, who advanced to meet Mrs. Warner.

Madame L'Ame was very much stunted in size, so much so as to appear almost a dwarf; and she looked shorter than she really was from a habit of constant stooping. She seldom raised her eyes from the ground, but moved them restlessly to and fro, as if always searching for something on the floor. Her mouth, which she usually kept a little open, had a vacant, silly expression; which gave Jessy an idea, at first sight, that the lady possessed a very small share of sense. The young girl was confirmed in this impression by Madame L'Ame's conduct during the whole of the visit.

Notwithstanding the very serious and important business upon which Mrs. Warner soon entered—business which concerned the lady's title to succeed to an immense property, and even her claim to all that she then possessed—Madame L'Ame appeared as though she thought the subject not worthy a moment's attention. She was constantly interrupting Mrs. Warner with some frivolous remark which had nothing to do with the question at issue. She was far more taken up with the tricks and gambols of Plaisir, her petted and pampered monkey, than she was with business on which might depend her future wealth or absolute beggary. The screen also occupied much of her attention, and Madame L'Ame often interrupted the flow of her childish gossip to give directions to the maid about placing the pictures upon it.

"My dear Madame," said Mrs. Warner, earnestly, after concluding a statement which would have appeared interesting to any one but the person chiefly concerned, "it is now high time for you to take a decided part. Your enemies are powerful and active, your claim doubtful—"

"Now, does he not look droll?" exclaimed Madame L'Ame, who had twisted a gauze scarf over the head of her favourite, and was laughing at his efforts to free himself from his veil.

"Really this is no time for trifling," said the visitor, "when so much is at stake; I have been informed that—"

"Mabel, Mabel!" cried the lady to her maid, "bring these dancing figures more to the front—there! and the coloured flowers to form a pretty border round them!" and she started up from her seat to show the exact spot on the screen which she wished to have decorated by the woodcuts.

Mrs. Warner's usually serene countenance showed signs of impatience and annoyance; they had quite passed away, however, before the lady returned to her seat.

"I really must beg for half an hour of your earnest, undivided attention," said the visitor. "I have walked some distance on purpose to let you know the full extent of the evil which threatens you."

Madame L'Ame's eyes were wandering curiously over the dress of Jessy—her bonnet, her bracelets, her flounces; and at the first pause in her visitor's address she inquired, "Pray, who is your milliner, my dear?"

Mrs. Warner rose in despair; she had given up all hope of engaging the mind of her weak and frivolous acquaintance on anything beyond the trifles of the hour. She quitted the apartment and the house, but not before Madame L'Ame had detailed to her all the petty gossip of the neighbourhood, and asked her opinion on various important subjects, such as the fit of a glove, or the tint of a riband.

"Mamma!" exclaimed Jessy, when they stepped out into the open air, glad to escape from society so insipid, "who would ever have believed Madame L'Ame to be the owner of so beautiful a house! Surely she is quite out of her mind!"

"She is weak in her intellect, I fear."

"Weak!—oh, mamma, I do not believe that she has any intellect at all! She seemed to think more of that monkey than of all the splendid fortune of which you were telling her; and I do believe that she would care more about losing a few of her paltry beads and pictures than for forfeiting a kingdom, if she had one. I never saw any one so silly!"

"Ah, my child," said Mrs. Warner, quietly, "let us take care that we ourselves are not betrayed into greater and more fatal folly. If it is sad to see the mere outward appearance alone regarded, the furnishing of the mind neglected, how much sadder to see *the soul*, unworthy mistress of a beautiful mansion, itself unlovely and stunted, devoted to trifles unworthy its regard, while its highest interests are forgotten! Have we never met with one to whom the most important of all subjects appeared tedious and uninteresting? who cared more for the amusement of the moment than the happiness of ages to come? whom serious conversation only wearied, though it might regard a future crown to be inherited or lost, and who would rather listen to any tale of idle gossip than to a message of *glad tidings* from heaven?"

Jessy walked home silent and reflecting. For the first time in her life she thought less of the "cottage of clay" which she had so delighted to adorn, than of the dweller therein, the immortal soul.

Many years passed away before Jessy had occasion again to revisit the beautiful villa embosomed in trees. It looked changed, for the season was that of winter. The lovely creepers showed neither blossoms nor leaves; the gilded pinnacle of the clock-tower had been blown down by a gale; but the clock itself had been long since repaired, and was keeping good time, and striking the hour on its silvery bell, like a brave spirit on a round of daily duty. And cheerfully blazed the fires in the neat and well-furnished rooms. Their former occupant had died in poverty many years before; her very memory had almost passed away from the place in which she had dwelt. A happy, united family, now inhabited the beautiful home; the ringing laugh of childhood was heard there, pleasant and sweet to the ear; but not so pleasant or sweet as the sound of the hymn which rose morning and eve from the happy abode, to Him from whom all happiness flows!

The house was much changed when Jessy revisited it; but Jessy herself was more changed than the house. The pretty child, as often happens, had not grown into the beautiful woman; and sickness, time, and care, had robbed her of all trace of good looks. The rounded cheek has become hollow, the rose-colour has faded, the sparkling eyes have lost all their brightness! And yet Jessy is now far more agreeable as a companion, and far more valuable as a friend; more loved in her family, more happy in her own mind, than she ever was when lovely and young. A gentle, cheerful, loving spirit dwells in the faded form, and sheds a light on homely features which makes them more than fair. The beauty which passes away like a flower is exchanged for *the beauty of holiness*, which never fades, which never dies, but finds its perfection in heaven! *Favour is deceitful, and beauty is vain: but a woman that feareth the Lord, she shall be praised.*

The unsightly shell

A pearl may enshrine,—

In homely form dwell

A spirit divine.

Oh! favour's deceitful,

And beauty is vain;

But virtue's the pearl

Which will precious remain!

The weed's scarlet dye

Outshineth the corn,

Yet gladdens no eye,

To no garner is borne.

Oh! favour's deceitful

And beauty is vain;

But virtue's rich harvest

Will precious remain!

What matters what hue

To the eye has been given,

If the soul that looks through

Wear the beauty of heaven!

Oh! favour's deceitful,

And comeliness vain;

But virtue for ever

Will lovely remain!

Milton Keynes UK
Ingram Content Group UK Ltd.
UKHW050238220624
444555UK00005BA/449

9 789361 479045